Patron of Hope

R. A. EMERSON

ISBN: 978-1-7368336-1-2

DEDICATION

This book is dedicated to my lovely wife Lori who demonstrates infinite patience with me every day. Without her love and support, none of this would be possible.

CONTENTS

1   Chapter One   10

2   Chapter Two   22

3   Chapter Three   28

4   Chapter Four   42

5   Chapter Five   47

6   Chapter Six   53

7   Chapter Seven   57

8   Chapter Eight   65

9   Chapter Nine   82

10   Chapter Ten   93

11   Chapter Eleven   101

12   Chapter Twelve   117

13   Chapter Thirteen   122

14   Chapter Fourteen   137

15   Chapter Fifteen   147

16   Chapter Sixteen   152

17   Chapter Seventeen   157

18	Chapter Eighteen	167
19	Chapter Nineteen	175
20	Chapter Twenty	181
21	Chapter Twenty-One	187
22	Chapter Twenty-Two	191
23	Chapter Twenty-Three	194
	Afterword	200
	About the Author	200

CHAPTER ONE
Marco

The subway doors opened, and Marco spilled out onto the platform along with dozens of his commuter companions. Bumping along like a pinball, he worked his way through the station. As the crowd thinned, Marco picked up his pace. He was in a hurry and moving with purpose as he reached the stairs to exit the subway station. He was on his way to the office, but not excited about getting there. Marco was a social worker for the city. He was on a team of first responders who were called on when someone dialed 911 to report a social disturbance. Sometimes it was a call about a mentally ill person. Sometimes it was a domestic dispute. It was usually something dangerous, and the people involved were rarely happy to see him. Sometimes he went out as a team of two, and Marco appreciated the backup. But more times than not, he went it alone.

Being on this unit was a highly coveted position within the Social Services Bureau. Unfortunately, by all measures, Marco shouldn't have been working in this department. He was the beneficiary of a special program that gave him a leg up in the application process. Some in the department used that against him. He didn't have the same pedigree or comparable credentials. As a result, he felt like the unit leadership gave him the undesirable calls. The calls no one else wanted to go on. The most dangerous ones in the worst neighborhoods. Marco didn't mind going into these neighborhoods, because he knew them well. Those were his streets. His home. He just wanted respect, damn it. He was as good as them, and they knew it.

One more corner and then one block to go. He was almost running now. His backpack was like a lead weight on his back. Marco didn't have a stellar attendance record at work. In fact, it was pretty poor, and he was afraid that if he showed up late again, they might fire him. He was in a union, but even they had almost given up on him. They didn't understand. He worked this job so he could afford to continue doing his real job. His foundation. Of course, he couldn't tell them that. So he had the usual arsenal of excuses why he was late to work or missed a day. Again.

No time to take the elevator. It was only on the third floor, so up the stairs he went, two at a time. He was in a full sweat now as he opened the stairwell door and stepped in front of the glass-paned door leading into his department. Marco swept back his long dark hair, dampened with sweat from his run, and smoothed out his jacket and pants. He quickly glanced at his watch. Five after nine. "Damn." Before he could grab the knob, the door flew open.

"Damn, Marco. Again? Get your butt in here." It was one of his coworkers. One of the few he actually liked, and he stepped aside to let Marco pass. The office was cavernous, loud, and buzzing with activity as he walked to his desk. People were rushing back and forth as phones rang on many of the desks in this converted brick building. Old fluorescent light tubes hung from the ceiling between large ventilation ducts and an exposed concrete ceiling. Old computers and even older telephones adorned the tops of creaky old desks that showed the department's lack of importance and the level of financial support it received within the city. The room was full of mostly young people, who had just started out in their careers. Young people with advanced degrees in psychology or social sciences who looked to make a name for themselves. They worked long hours in dangerous conditions. Sometimes they got hurt. Sometimes really badly.

Who else would work for these crappy wages? Marco thought as he approached his desk, slinging his backpack off his shoulder and setting it down with a thud. "Damn that smell. What is that?" Marco said to himself, as he did every day. "Mold, sweat, burned coffee... maybe a dead rat or two." All things considered, Marco disliked this job.

He spun his chair around, but before he could even sit, he felt a powerful tug on the back of his shirt. "The boss wants to see you." Marco turned to see another one of his coworkers. Frank. Marco hated Frank, and he knew the feeling was mutual. He and Frank had worked cases together in the past, and they rarely ended well. Marco got no respect from Frank. He was just like the rest of them around here. Frank had a smug look of self-satisfaction on his face as he delivered the message. "Now, Marco!"

"Yeah, I'm going," Marco mumbled under his breath as he turned around and spotted the boss's office at the other end of the floor. Marco's mind wandered, and he wondered if this was the day. Would they finally fire him? Were all the times he had stuck a figurative middle finger up to the system finally catching up with him? He felt the quality of his work was good, as were his results. He didn't understand why they got so hung up on him being at his desk at exactly nine.

As he got closer to the boss's door, he could hear the yelling inside, growing in intensity. That was Terry, and he was always yelling at someone. Usually it was Marco, but he took some comfort in knowing that someone else was getting trained in the role of the fall guy. Sweat covered Marco's hands as he knocked on the door. A booming, angry voice greeted him from inside, and demanded he come in. Marco opened the door and saw the usual carnage that was Terry's office: papers strewn everywhere, files piled up on the desk, garbage on the floor, two old torn armchairs in front of his desk, with Mike Sever standing bolt upright between them. Mike was a new employee, and it was obvious the boss was giving him a pep talk. Terry's voice matched his larger-than-life size and personality. He was intimidating and enjoyed it. His white-collar shirt was stained with something Marco thought was the meatball sandwich he ate last week. His face was red, especially his nose, and his oversized jowls bounced as he spoke. He quickly dismissed Mike, who moved past in a flash, turning his steely gaze toward Marco.

Slam! The door closed behind him, and Marco knew it was him and the lion and only a desk between them. He tentatively walked up to take the place of the previous victim. Terry looked like he was ready to pounce, and Marco thought, *Just fire me and get it over with.* He felt for the arm of the chair and turned to sit, never taking his eyes off the big cat just five feet away.

"Don't bother sitting down! This won't take long," Terry growled. The smell of his breath rolled across the open space like a San Francisco fog. When it reached Marco, he became nauseous. Halitosis accented by coffee, and whatever Terry had had for breakfast, the leftovers of which were still in a carryout tin on his desk. It was the worst breath Marco had ever smelled.

"You need to go back over to the Sixty-Eighth place. Where you went last week. We have another complaint that someone is hurting that baby and her mom. Get to the bottom of it this time! I don't want another kid getting hurt. That kind of attention from the press is terrible for us all! You understand?"

Marco nodded his head in understanding, but it was never enough for Terry. "I didn't hear you!" As he stood up behind his desk, the chair rolled out from under him and crashed into the wall behind with a thud. He leaned in, closing the distance to within two feet.

Marco squeaked out a "yes," then cleared his throat and

gave a slightly more confident "Yes, I understand, chief."

"Then what are you doing still standing there?" he said, thrusting a case folder in his direction. Marco grabbed it, spun around, and sprinted to the door. As he got there, he heard Terry, who was intent on throwing one last rock at Marco before he left. "Don't think I didn't see you walking in late again today! You are about this close..." But the door muffled his voice as Marco slammed it on him in mid-sentence. Marco stopped on the other side of the door and took a deep breath. He put his hand behind his back and gave the now closed door the middle finger and walked away.

***

The bus rolled on toward his stop as Marco reviewed the documentation in the file folder given to him by Terry. Marco was extremely familiar with this case. He had been to this house several times when various members of the community called to report potential abuse. Andrea lived there with Tanya, her three-year-old daughter. She was twenty-two and had a long history of meth and heroin abuse. Besides Tanya, Andrea had two other children. Sadly, they were both lost. One temporarily placed with the state and the other lost forever to violence. Marco had met many other houseguests during his visits. They preferred to stay unidentified. These were drifters, ex-cons, or other addicts who camped out there. Of all the people he had encountered there, Marco was only genuinely afraid of one. His name was Sam, and he was a mountain of a man with an equally large temper. According to Andrea, he was her boyfriend. When he wasn't living with Andrea, he was staying, for various lengths of time, at the nearby county correctional facility.

Marco replaced the file folder in his backpack and stepped off the bus. Just four houses over and he arrived at his destination. As he walked up onto the porch, he scanned the surroundings. He was familiar with this type of community and knew the risks of being there. Over the years, he had gotten good at protecting himself. He had only ever been hurt one time, and that wasn't his fault.

The lawn, at least what was growing between the weeds, hadn't been cut in quite some time. The porch was barely standing and needed painting badly. One of the front bay windows had been broken since the last time he was here. Most likely by a stray bullet. Several gangs had lain claim to this neighborhood as their territory, so shootings were common. He knocked on the door and immediately heard an explosion of barking dogs inside. Marco listened intently but couldn't hear any movement inside the house. At least not of the human kind. He leaned around and peeked inside the house through the broken window. No one yet. He knocked again and the dog activity reached a fever pitch. He briefly considered going around back and looking in, but that would have been an especially risky move. People in the area didn't like it when they saw strangers in their yards looking in the windows. Everyone looked out for each other and you just might get a baseball bat across your head or a bullet in the back. A third knock finally brought the sounds of a person who had probably tired of the incessant dog barking. Marco saw the curtain move and a single eye peered out at him.

"Hi, Andrea. It's Marco from Social Services."

The door cracked open ever so slightly. "Marco, you know I don't need you comin' round here none. Makin' trouble for me. You know Sam's out and he's not gonna be happy if he catches you here."

A wave of fear washed over Marco with the mention of Sam's name. "Sorry, Andrea, we received more calls so I have to come in. You know how this works."

The eye in the window disappeared, and Marco could hear Andrea yelling at the dogs. An interior door closed, then the front door opened ever so slowly until there was just enough room for Marco to slip in. The house was almost unfit for habitation. It was dark, and he was sure there wasn't any electricity. There probably wasn't any running water, either. Looking up, he could see water damage all across the ceiling with parts of it missing down the hall. The tattered carpet was worn down to the threads and large holes dotted the walls like a lunar landscape. There was an old mattress laying against the wall, a sofa against the other wall, and two mismatched wooden chairs. And the smell... Marco told his coworkers it was something you had to experience. *Putrid* was a word he had used in the past to describe it. That seemed appropriate. Andrea didn't seem pleased to have Marco here and continued to stand while Marco took up a seat in one of the chairs.

"What do you want?" she said as Marco inventoried her features and mannerisms. The court had ordered her to stop doing drugs, but from the look of things, she hadn't complied. Andrea was five feet four but weighed barely ninety pounds. She appeared sickly, and as he looked her over, she burst out, "What? I'm not doing drugs anymore, okay? Stop looking at me!" Marco gave her a warm smile and invited her to sit in the other chair.

As she moved into the light that shown through the window, he got a better look at her. Her dark hair was matted with light colored streaks that looked a lot like dried vomit. She wore a neon green T-shirt with many large stains and a pair of yellow terrycloth shorts that exposed her bony legs. In the light, Marco saw dozens of open sores all over her body and as she sat down and crossed her legs, she picked at one of them. Her eyes were sunk deep into her head and darted around the room briefly before settling back onto Marco. Her eyes were dilated, and he saw the remnants of teeth inside her mouth. She looked like a living corpse.

"You can be honest with me, Andrea, are you still doing meth?" He gave her a soft look and tried to build a therapeutic relationship with her. During past visits, she had been hesitant to talk to him. "You need help, Andrea. I can get you help. You can trust me."

"Honest, I ain't done no drugs since the court said no. I don't want to lose my little girl." She began to cry as she crossed and uncrossed her legs multiple times. Her eyes continued to dart around as tears rolled down her face.

Marco opened his backpack and took out a small package of tissues, handing one to Andrea. He wasn't buying her game, but he had to earn her trust. In the file folder, he removed a group of papers that were stapled together and tried to hand them to Andrea. "These are the names of the places I told you about. You need to get help before it's too late."

In a split second, the speed of which surprised Marco, Andrea stood up, moved over to his chair, and got within inches of his face. "I told you before, if I leave, Sam will kill me! And if he doesn't kill me, he will for sure hurt my girl! I can't do it!" He thought back to his experiences he had had with meth addicts. They could turn on you in an instant, but he remained calm.

"Please sit back down," he said, pointing to the chair. He had to admit that her actions took him by surprise. While he wasn't afraid of her, she could have done some damage if provoked. She eased back into the chair as he pointed in his backpack and told her, "I'm supposed to administer a drug test that I have in here, but I won't do it if you tell me what you are on, okay?" It was a bluff. He didn't have the authority to do that, or the means, but she didn't know it.

"Okay, okay. I just did a little meth that Sam got for me. Nothing else, I promise."

"Where is Sam?" Marco asked, finding that his eyes were now darting around the room at the smallest sound.

"I don't know. He left two days ago and I haven't seen him since," Andrea said as her eyes seemed to soften some. Marco thought his previous time with her might have paid off.

"Has he beat you, Andrea?" Marco asked but got no response. "Andrea, it's not your fault he does that. Does he hit you?"

"He don't mean it. It's the drugs. They make him do it. He's a good man," Andrea said, and this was the most open admission he had ever heard from her.

Marco dared to hope they might have a breakthrough here today. He thought about how nice it would have been to throw that back in Terry's face tomorrow. He had no confidence in him. No bad press was going to come from this visit. Not today. Then he looked into Andrea's eyes and was immediately ashamed of himself. He let his anger with Terry get the best of him. This was about Andrea and Tanya getting help, not his petty squabble at work. But Marco was jarred from his moment of introspection by a sound behind him. He realized that he had let his guard down and put himself in a difficult position. His back was to the hallway and the rest of the house, making it almost impossible to see anyone approaching from the back door. His heart skipped a beat as he stood up and whirled around.

"There's my baby!" Andrea shouted as Marco saw a small figure scurry past him. The shock caused him to take two steps back, but embarrassment quickly took over as he realized the commotion was from Tanya, now wrapped in her mom's arms.

It took a few minutes, but Marco regained his composure enough to continue with the interview. Before he did, though, he picked his chair up and moved it to a better position. One where he could see down the hall and also make his way to the front door if an escape became necessary. He felt stupid to not have done that at the beginning, but he comforted himself by thinking, *No harm, no foul.*

Marco looked over at the small child now sitting in her mother's lap. She was thin like her mother. Too thin. Her hair was long and tangled, partially covering her pretty face and deep brown eyes. Tanya peered out through clumps of hair and gave Marco a smile. She had seen him here before and was not afraid. Tanya was wearing a filthy nightdress with Minnie Mouse printed on the front. He knew the chances of her seeing the real thing were extremely remote. Marco noticed a cast on her right arm and tried remembering if that was a recent injury to Tanya since his last visit.

"What happened to her arm?" Marco inquired.

"She done fell down playin' last week," Andrea responded, with a sheepish look that gave away the truth of her daughter's injury. Andrea's eyes began darting around again as she continued to scratch at her legs. Marco considered that it's possible, but unlikely that she was injured while playing. A picture of Sam flashed in his mind.

"Andrea. We need to get you and Tanya to a safe place where you can get help." As Marco said these words, Tanya reached out her cast-covered arm toward him. He took her tiny hand in his. Looking down, he noticed the file folder had fallen on the floor and picked it up. He opened it and removed the stapled papers with resource information on them and handed them to Andrea. This time she reached out and took them.

"I can't leave. I have nowhere else to go," she mumbled.

Then a noise in the backyard. Hardly noticeable at first, it caused Andrea to turn her head and look down the hall. When her head snapped back toward Marco, there was a look of terror in her eyes. "He's back. You have to leave! Now!" Her words had barely registered with Marco when the back door crashed open. It was too far down the hall to see, but Marco knew what, or who, was coming and began to panic. He knew there were only a few seconds for him to react. Looking around, he assessed his situation. His mind told him he should leave, but his heart made him stay. Despite the risks to his safety, he couldn't abandon Tanya and Andrea. He was making good progress with her and felt like he could help them get to a safe place. He remained seated. Andrea was up in a second and met him as he entered the room, putting her slight frame in front of Sam and impeding his entry farther into the living room.

"'Bout time you got home. Where you been?" Andrea said, craning her neck to look up at Sam's face.

"Taking care of business. What the hell does it matter to you!" Sam retorted and pushed Andrea aside with the effort it would have taken to swat away a mosquito.

Sam looked around the room, and his eyes settled on Marco, still calmly seated in the chair. "What are you doing here?" There was agitation in his voice. He seemed paranoid, and Marco suspected he was high. His heart was beating in his throat, his hands were now moist with sweat, and he was shaking a little with nervousness. But Marco had been in situations like this before and knew he had to stand his ground. Sam was incredibly restless, almost bouncing from one leg to the other. Back and forth in ceaseless motion. Meth. On the mattress against the wall, Tanya had crawled under a blanket and was hiding, her big brown eyes visible through a space in the blanket. She had seen this play many times before, and it scared her. Sam slowly walked over to Marco, who, from outward appearances, seemed unconcerned. The floorboards creaked under his weight as he took a position directly in front of Marco.

"Who are you, little man?" Sam said in a menacing voice.

"My name is Marco, and I work for the state. I'm here doing a wellness check on Andrea and Tanya. You are welcome to join us, if you'd like."

"I'd say we're all looking well, so you can leave right now before I make you sorry you came."

"You have enough trouble in your life, Sam. I wouldn't go out of my way to create any more," Marco replied, trying to appear calm.

Sam turned and redirected his attention toward Andrea, who was still holding the paperwork she had taken from Marco. He reached out, snatching it from her hands. "What is this?" he asked, directing his anger at Andrea.

Marco knew that standing up to confront Sam could create an escalation of the conflict, but he had to step in to keep Andrea safe. He stood up and took a step toward Sam, trying to make himself taller than his six-foot frame. He could see that Sam had him by several inches.

"What do you think you're gonna do?" Sam asked as he turned his head toward Marco. But before anyone could answer, a car came to a stop outside, and a horn sounded several times.

"Today is your lucky day, little man," Sam snorted as he made his way to the front door, intentionally bumping his shoulder into Marco's chest as he passed.

As Sam went out the door, he flung the papers he had snatched from Andrea, and they fluttered to the floor. Marco walked over and picked them up. After watching Sam get into a red sedan in the street, he made his way back to Andrea.

"Please let us help you," he told her, extending his hand to give her the papers.

"You need to go," she said.

Marco was relieved when she took them from him. He kneeled down next to the mattress in front of the tiny eyes that continued to peer out from under the blanket. Slowly he uncovered Tanya and extended his hand to her. She took it, and he helped her up.

He smiled at her, and she smiled back. Marco stood up, making one last plea before leaving. "Call me if you need anything."

He left without knowing if his efforts would pay off or not. Andrea needed help, and time was running out. She took the papers, which was a good sign, and he hoped they would guide her to a safe place. Marco knew that it took many attempts before people changed their lives. *Baby steps,* he said to himself as he walked to the bus stop. It was a long shot, but he had a good feeling about it.

CHAPTER TWO
Victoria

The sleek black Mercedes purred as it inched its way down the cobblestone driveway toward the metal gates adorned with *VH*. These gates had protected the family compound for decades. Years ago, there was always a security guard at the gate, but now, with advances in electronic surveillance, it was an unnecessary luxury. Still, Victoria felt more secure in those days. *What good would it do to see the bad guys coming if there was no one there to stop them?* she wondered to herself as she pushed the button. The heavy gates swung open, and she turned right, leaving the 20,000-square-foot mansion behind. It usually took about thirty minutes to get to work, so she settled in for the drive.

Victoria was a student of observation and enjoyed people-watching the most. As she stopped at the first traffic light, she noted the things going on around her. In her rearview mirror was a man dressed in a business suit who appeared to be yelling to no one in particular. Probably talking on his cell phone. It caused her to think of her father. She had many fond thoughts of him and knew he would never conduct business in that way. Victoria learned everything she knew about business from him, and she didn't yell, either. Her people got things done, or they went to work for someone else. Simple.

At the next light, Victoria noticed a woman with three children in the car. She stared at them, all well behaved. Each one was occupying themselves with a video game of some sort, and Victoria approved. She guessed they had an especially strong mother who taught them manners and respect. For a minute, Victoria found herself thinking about a family of her own. She wanted to have children, and of course a husband, but this was more complicated than she ever imagined. When you had money, you were strongly encouraged to marry money. At least that was what her mother insisted. Over the years, she had been fixed up with many men. All hand chosen by her mother. All successful business executives, but all relationship failures, in Victoria's opinion. Now that she was in her thirties, there was more of a sense of urgency to her search. She would love to find a man who wanted to be a partner with her. One who was as intellectual as she and as driven for success as she was. Most importantly, though, Victoria wanted a man who appreciated her little quirks. She loved to have fun. She loved playing tricks on people and seeing the look on their faces when it was over. She loved to laugh. She wanted... no, *needed* a man who loved her for who she was. Of course, there had been one man. Nate. But he wasn't in her life anymore. So other than him, she was zero for God-knows-how-many.

The light turned green and off she went again, turning onto the freeway. She wasn't sure why she was always in such a hurry to get to work, because she hated that her mother was the president and Victoria did all the work. *Actually*, she thought, *that position should have been mine.* She turned the radio up to rock concert levels to rid her brain of these thoughts and enjoyed the music for the final few miles until her arrival.

Victoria pulled into a spot marked *Executive VP* and switched the car off. Her spot was right next to the front door. *Perks of the job*, she thought. She pulled the visor down one last time and examined herself in the mirror before blowing herself a kiss and closing it. She took a deep breath and exited the car. The neon sign on the building read *Van Hough Industries, Inc.* This was the company her father built from nothing: importers of fine consumables. She opened the door and entered the sleek, modern reception area decorated with the finest, high-end furnishings. The receptionist was there and greeted her cordially, "Good morning, Ms. Van Hough." Victoria believed in being polite to everyone and so she bade her a "good morning," but moved on quickly with no extraneous conversation. Down the hall, she passed the desk where her assistant, Paige, sat, and she greeted her as well. Paige snapped to attention as Victoria passed and followed her into the adjoining office.

Consistent with the reception area, Victoria's office was impeccably decorated as well. Beautiful high-end photographs adorned the walls. Each one depicted either her or her father in action, on-site, picking out some of the fine products they imported. Her father in Peru, Colombia, and Greece, she in Brazil, Guatemala, and South Africa. Near the back of the office there was an oversized mahogany desk with matching credenzas. The office was enormous by most standards, but these items took up a large footprint within the room. Victoria sat down in the oversized chair, turned on the lights, and started her computer. Besides the desk, there were two fine leather high-back chairs that sat across from Victoria's desk. Paige stood between them at attention. Finally, several display cases, placed in strategic spots within the office, contained samples of many of the products they imported.

Van Hough Industries was an importer of the finest coffees, brandy, scotch, teas, olive oils, and nuts found anywhere in the world. All hand selected by her and her father before her. Victoria's job frequently took her to some of the most exotic locations on the planet. Then why did she feel so unmotivated? So detached? Part of the problem, she often admitted, was that her mother was the president of the company. Victoria knew she did all the work and her mother did nothing. The position passed to her when her father died. Victoria was too young to take over the company, so it made sense back then. Since that time,

Victoria had proven herself to be more than capable of taking over, but her mother wouldn't give up the position. She resented her for that because she knew her father was grooming her for the job. He told her so. All the trips they had taken together, the MBA, all the teaching made sure she could someday take over. She was so caught up in her disappointment that she didn't realize that Paige was waiting for her to respond. "Victoria? Did you hear what I asked?" she said.

"I'm sorry, Paige. What did you say?" Victoria said, feeling a little embarrassed that she was so spaced out.

"I put the latest contracts on your desk for review, and Mr. Jenkins would like a call back first thing this morning. Would you like a cup of coffee?" Paige said, taking advantage of having Victoria's undivided attention.

"Thanks, Paige, and yes please on the coffee," Victoria replied and immediately refocused on the paperwork sitting on her desk. As Paige left the office, another person shuffled in. Victoria was oblivious to the exchange and continued looking over the paperwork. After a few minutes, her unknown visitor made a sound like clearing her throat. Victoria looked up to see her best friend, Sue. They greeted each other with a warm smile. "I'm ordering out lunch. Do you want me to order anything for you?" Sue inquired.

"Sue... I haven't even had my cup of coffee yet and you're already talking about lunch. I'm going to need to book an extra appointment with my trainer if I hang out with you anymore."

They both laughed, and Sue said, "I'll order the usual for you. See you at noon," before walking out as Victoria dedicated herself to the work at hand.

***

Victoria walked into the conference room just as Sue was unpacking the food she had delivered for lunch. "Hey, Vic... here is your food," she said and slid two containers to the far side of the table.

"Thanks," she replied and sat down. Sue was her best friend. They had worked together for the past ten years, rising through the ranks from stocking the shelves and sweeping the warehouse floors to Victoria's position as executive vice president and Sue as director of information technology. They had supported each other through work and personal problems. Victoria would probably admit that Sue was more a support to her than she was to Sue. But not for a lack of trying. She just didn't always understand the problems that Sue was having. Sue had been married, then divorced, and had one child already, while Victoria had none of those things. Victoria had a hard time advising her without experience in these areas. Plus, Victoria didn't have money problems... except for her mother saying she spent too much of it.

"I'm not overly hungry today," Victoria said. This was code for *I have a problem*, and Sue recognized it.

"Alright, Vic, what's wrong?" she asked. Sue was the only person in the world who could call her anything except Victoria.

"I don't know. Nothing... everything. My mother is still pushing Stewart on me and he is a total dud." She looked out the door before continuing in a squeaky voice meant to mimic her mother. "'But, Victoria dear, he went to Yale, and his family is a member of our country club.'" Sue rolled her eyes while Victoria continued, "He just wants a woman on his arm. Sue, they are all the same. It's so maddening. Where can I find a man who wants to be a partner with me?" Victoria implored. It frustrated her.

"I don't know what to tell you except..." Sue looked around for prying eyes and ears before she continued. She whispered, "Stop taking advice from your mother. But don't tell her I said that. I need my job." She laughed uncomfortably. "Listen, Vic, you have great instincts. You find products from all over the world and turn them into bestsellers for us. Even ones where the entire team disagrees. But it all comes from your gut. You say 'screw it' and just do it. You need to do the same thing with a man," Sue said, then between bites, provided a list of things she must do to be successful. "Trust yourself... Trust your heart... Be spontaneous... Take chances."

"Sue, it's not that easy," Victoria said as she sighed with each new suggestion.

"It is!" Sue replied. "You can do it! Start this weekend. Don't wait."

"Oh, hell. I wish I could. This weekend, I'm going to a fundraiser with my mother. Boring! She's trying to get me to go to these functions more often, but I hate them. All these socialites walking around talking about how they are changing the world. 'I'm supporting the rain forests... I'm reducing my carbon footprint,'" Victoria mocked the fictitious attendees. "Ugh! So pretentious! They drive me crazy."

"Give it a chance, Vic!" Sue responded and gave her most supportive face possible. "You have to kiss a lot of frogs before you find your prince."

Victoria wrapped her fingers around her throat and pretended to squeeze, and they both laughed. Deep down, Victoria knew that she didn't have a choice. Her mother made it abundantly clear that she was going with her whether she liked it or not. What Victoria didn't know was that this fundraiser could be different. Vastly different.

CHAPTER THREE
Marco

The black limousine made its way through the crowded downtown streets one traffic light at a time. This was the most affluent part of town, and limos were a common sight here. High rises with million-dollar condos, museums, and restaurants where a meal costs more than most people make in a week all dotted the streets. Marco sat in the back and worked through his game plan for the evening. He hated spending precious foundation money on such a luxury, but it was a necessary evil. In a few minutes, he would arrive at the Fleisher Ball and Auction. It was the second most important fundraising event in the city, and Marco had to show up in style. They would expect it. It was all about appearances, and you had to appear as though you belong in high society. People paid attention. They saw how you arrived and were already judging you before you even stepped out of the car. Getting there in style was a good start, but it was only the price of admission. If Marco expected to get a check, he needed to fit in. He needed to become one of them. It was a game he played, and he was pretty good at it. He thought of himself as a modern-day superhero. Mild-mannered social worker by day, sexy, stylish do-gooder by night with superpowers that got rich people to donate money to his foundation. He saw himself as a cross between Robin Hood and Superman. The thought of that made him happy. They were all so damn pretentious. But he needed them, and in a way, they needed people like him to feel good about themselves. To be able to tell their friends they were helping society. "Look at me. I donated to this charity or that foundation," they told their friends. "I'm saving the rain forests." "I'm reducing my carbon footprint." Marco thought they could tell their friends whatever they wanted as long as their checks cleared. Marco knew that if he made a hundred million dollars, he would still never live in their world. He didn't fit in there.

The limo stopped in front of the city aquarium. It was a beautiful building that just underwent a ten-million-dollar renovation, funded by wealthy contributors. Now those contributors wanted their payback. It was their playground for the night. They took private tours in areas where most people never went. Fed animals that the public couldn't. *Typical*, Marco thought. Many of those events took place in locations like this. What said money more than to close the aquarium on a busy Saturday night. Marco stepped out into the crisp fall air. He was presenting himself to the rich gods. Appearance only began with the limo, and Marco understood that as he looked down at his black-and-white tuxedo, nicely pressed with a perfectly tied bow tie. Marco's hair was gelled back, and he was wearing expensive cologne that fit the night. *Or is it* eau de toilette? he wondered and laughed a little. He couldn't care less. He knew he looked every bit as good as anyone else in that building, and he was confident he would score tonight.

He slowly made his way up the marble stairs to the front entrance, being careful to time his arrival for when he was alone at the large double doors. There was a method to his madness.

"Hey," Marco said to the man stationed at the front door. He had a clipboard and an earphone in his ear and controlled access into the event.

"Welcome to this evening's event. May I have your name please, sir?" said the young, thin man guarding the door.

"Marco DeFranco," he replied as the man scanned the guest list attached to his clipboard. He looked down at the first page, then the second, and finally the last. He stopped, looked up at Marco, and reviewed the list one more time.

"I'm sorry, Mr. DeFranco. Your name is not on my list. I can't let you in," came the response.

A heavy scowl developed over Marco's face and he began feeling flush. "Seriously, man. You're gonna do this to me tonight?" Marco replied in a somewhat annoyed voice.

The doorman reached up and fiddled with his earphone as if he were getting ready to call for backup. Then he smiled. "Aw, I'm just messing with you, dude. Lighten up." He turned the sheet of paper over to the blank side and said, "I see your name is right here, Mr. DeFranco. Go right in. Have a wonderful time."

A look of relief washed over Marco's face. "I knew you were messing with me. Is Allison here yet?"

"Yep. She got here a few minutes ago."

Marco shook his hand, but no one saw the hundred-dollar bill that passed from his hand to the doorman's. Marco has done favors for many people and got many favors in return.

Through the double doors he went. The architecture impressed Marco. The main hall was immense, with a cement walking path that wound up and around the biggest cylindrical fish tank he had ever seen. It was four stories tall and was the centerpiece of the aquarium. At each level, the walking path flattened out to allow visitors a chance to rest. For this event, tables serving either beverages or food occupied each of the platforms. In the aquarium, Marco made mental notes about several exotic fish that swam around inside. He repeated the names to himself, "Platinum Arowana, polka-dot stingray, peppermint angelfish." He had spent many nights at the library researching the fish of this aquarium. It was an excellent conversation starter and showed that he was cultured. As he weaved his way through the throngs of people, he craned his neck to see some of the rarest specimens swimming toward the top, just as his shoulder landed squarely into someone's back. Marco turned in time to see a young woman stumble forward as her handbag went flying and her small plate of food flew out of her hand, landing on the cement floor with a crash. With lightning-fast reflexes, he reached forward, grabbing her arm in time to steady her.

"Oh my gosh, I'm so sorry," Marco exclaimed as the woman turned around. As she looked at him, her scowl turned into a smile. It was electric, and she was stunning.

"No problem. It's a crowded place," she said, with a squeeze of his arm for reassurance.

Marco walked over and retrieved her handbag, giving it back to the beautiful stranger.

"Are you sure you're okay?"

"I'm fine, really," she said, taking her handbag back. "Hope to see you around," she said as she turned and walked away. Initially he resisted the urge to turn around and watch her, but soon, the temptation became too great. While pretending to scan the room, he glanced behind him to see where the beautiful stranger went. But much to his disappointment, she had vanished into the crowd.

He returned his gaze forward and continued making his way through the main hall toward the giant aquarium. At the base of the ramp, there were concrete benches and Marco took a seat on one of them. He sat next to a thin blond woman several years his junior. She was dressed impeccably in a bright red cocktail dress and her hair was styled in an intricate pattern across her head, ending in a ponytail. Most men would have called her a looker, but Marco never saw her that way.

"Glad to see you made it," she said to Marco, never looking over at him.

"Arriving is all about timing," Marco said, trying to

educate her. "There is a pecking order for these events, and you have to do it just right."

"Does 'just right' mean taking out a guest?" she asked with a smirk. "Who did you manage to run over? I couldn't see the show."

"Hilarious. So, what do you have so far?" Marco asked, getting right down to business. Allison was the first and only employee of his foundation. He paid her, but not well. His love for saving the world only went so far. The size of her salary ensured she lived an exceedingly Spartan lifestyle, just like Marco, and the rest of the money in the foundation went toward doing good. Allison didn't understand why Marco lived the way he did. She didn't have to understand. She just had to do a good job, which she did in spades.

"I saw the Keens in the exhibit to the left over there. Ingrid Johnson is hanging up her coat right now. A really expensive designer number, I might add," Allison recited.

"Did you find Mrs. Van Hough yet?" Marco inquired. This was his number one target for the evening. He had spoken to her briefly before and thought he could finally crack open her checkbook tonight.

"She's up on the third level above us. But she's with someone I've never seen before. A pretty young woman in a nice little Oscar de la Renta dress. She has good taste," Allison said with a grin.

"Good. Keep an eye on the Keens and I'm going up to the third level."

"Of course you are," she said with a bit of derision in her voice.

"What does that mean?" Marco asked.

"I had you at 'pretty' and 'young.' But remember, I said she has good taste. That leaves you out in the cold. Sorry."

"I'm here for business, not to get a date. You should keep that in mind." Marco snarled as he stood up and headed to the ramp going to the third floor. Sometimes he just didn't understand Allison. He was extremely knowledgeable regarding psychology but struggled with his understanding of her. Her inappropriate comments came at the worst times. He thought she really needed to get her relationship with her boyfriend back on track.

As Marco took the long walk to the third floor, he looked in the large, beautiful aquarium and continued with his mental exercise of inventorying the fish he saw: bladefin basslet, Neptune grouper, masked angelfish. *The masked angelfish starts out as a female and will eventually turn into a male*, he said to himself, trying out some of the more interesting information he had learned. At the first landing, he noted a table set up serving food and went over to review the selection. He didn't have time to eat, and his stomach was letting him know through a symphony of sounds. He looked at the offering and saw that it was almost exclusively high-end sushi. He took a plate and placed several pieces on it before placing a small tip in the jar. Then he turned around and headed toward the ramp. Marco placed the first piece of sushi in his mouth as he looked into the tank and laughed. *How ironic. Eating sushi in an aquarium*, he said to himself with a chuckle. He held up a piece to the glass as a fish swam by. *Anyone you know?*

Off he went again, circling the aquarium as he ascended to the next landing. This time the station was serving drinks. There were the usual alcoholic varieties available: bourbon sours, martinis, and a favorite of Queen Elizabeth's, gin and Dubonnet. Marco ordered up a Diet Coke. Nothing else. He didn't drink alcohol. Ever. He was keenly aware of the dangers that drugs and alcohol presented. He saw it in a painfully personal way with his father as he circled the drain of life, and he had no intentions of repeating the same mistakes. Plus, he was working tonight, and he needed a big score.

As he approached the third landing, he scanned the area for his target, Mrs. Van Hough. She was relatively easy to spot, Marco thought. A late middle-aged woman with an impeccable body, honed by many hours of gym time with her personal trainer and a diet carefully crafted by the best personal chefs that money could buy. She obviously had a close relationship with some of the best plastic surgeons in the country as well. Undoubtedly, she was wearing one of those Oscar-de-la-so-and-so dresses that Allison cared so much about. He educated himself on more appropriate things. Things that got him closer to his goal. A check.

As if on cue, she appeared in front of him, looking into the clear water as several schools of fish swam by. She seemed to be alone. *Timing is everything*, Marco thought as he set his plate down, put a mint in his mouth, and eased over to quietly stand beside her. Marco knew that she would not engage him. He had to be the one to start the conversation, so he waited for his opening. As a long white fish swam by, he saw his chance. "I really enjoy watching the platinum Arowana swim. So elegant. Their beautiful color results from a rare genetic defect." Marco played his first card and let it hang out there to see if he got a response. Nothing. He tried again. "They come from Asia and are believed to boost health, luck, and prosperity."

Finally, a reaction. She turned toward Marco, gave him a forced smile, and said, "I know. I paid for that one. And all I got was a little plaque over on the wall with my name on it. You would think I would have gotten more for my four hundred grand, right?" She turned her attention back to the aquarium. Marco's hopes sunk a little. This wasn't starting out as well as he had wanted.

Then, she turned back to him and said, "I wonder what they taste like," and gave Marco a large, toothy grin. He knew she was pulling his leg now, but that was a good sign to him. Progress.

He laughed. "If you made your way to Asia, you may be able to find out."

"I love traveling to Asia. Those are some of my favorite countries," she said, and Marco made a mental note about how she lit up when saying that. Travel... one of her passions.

"My name is Marco DeFranco," he said, extending his

hand to her.

She declined to take it, but responded, "Yes, I know. We spoke before, I believe, about a month or two ago. You made a recommendation on a place to get my Bentley repaired." Marco was both excited and disappointed by her response. She remembered the conversation, but not his foundation. *At least she remembers me*, he reminded himself.

"How did that work out for you?" he asked.

"Excellent. They serve champagne while you wait," she said while turning to watch the fish again.

Marco tried to keep the conversation going. It was way too early to discuss his foundation. "You said you love traveling to Asia? I love that part of the world as well," he said, knowing that he had never been outside the U.S.

"Really?" she said, turning and looking him right in the eyes. She took a few seconds to look him up and down before finishing. "I didn't take you as an international traveler. What is your favorite country to visit?"

Marco saw this as a test. Pick the wrong country and the conversation could have been over. Marco thought for a minute, then responded, "Vietnam. By far." He saw a sparkle in her eyes, and he knew he hit pay dirt.

"Oh, I adore that country. So beautiful. And the people are just lovely. I used to travel there often with my late husband."

"I'm sorry," Marco blurted out reflexively at the reference to a deceased spouse.

"Don't be. He was a womanizing bastard. Left me with a daughter to raise. But I wouldn't have done it any other way. That young woman is the light of my life. Anyway..." She trailed off and went back to looking at the fish. Marco thought, *A passion?* That was a little unusual. For many of the ultra-wealthy, kids were anything but a passion. They were raised by nannies, then sent off to expensive boarding schools.

"And here she is now. Darling...I'm over here," Mrs. Van Hough said as she turned to face a young woman coming up the ramp toward her with two drinks in her hand. Marco was shocked to see it was the same woman he had the run-in with earlier. She seemed to walk on air as she made her way to them.

"I'd introduce you to her, but it seems you have already run into her," said Mrs. Van Hough.

The woman smiled again as she arrived at her mother's side. "Oh, Mother. It was an accident." Then she turned her attention to Marco. "How nice to see you again. I'm Victoria Van Hough, and of course you already know my mother." He examined her more closely now and was overtaken by her beauty. Her perfectly formed facial features and porcelain skin complemented her deep blue eyes. He couldn't take his eyes off her, but he also saw that hers seemed to be locked onto him as well.

The moment was broken by Mrs. Van Hough. "Nevertheless, you would be advised to pay better attention to where you are walking. My Victoria is all I have left in this world, and I'm very protective of her." She continued, "Victoria... I'd like you to meet Mr... ." She hesitated while trying to remember his last name.

"DeFranco," Marco said. "But call me Marco."

"He's the one who helped me get the Bentley fixed. He runs some kind of foundation here in the city," she said in a way that almost sounded dismissive.

"How wonderful! Tell me about your foundation, Mr. DeFranco."

"Well, um..." Being thrust directly into the limelight took Marco by surprise. He had what he often referred to as his elevator speech memorized. He used this when he had twenty seconds in an elevator to give someone a pitch. But this time, he seemed to stumble. Her poise and confidence impressed him, but also seemed to have left him tongue-tied. He quickly recovered and told her about how the money he collected was distributed by his foundation to help the lowest members of society. The forgotten ones. In fact, that was the name of his foundation, he told her. He relayed one of his success stories to her, and she listened intently, locked onto him with her steel-blue eyes. She was hanging on to his every word and nodded appropriately. This made Marco a little uncomfortable. He was used to watching people fumble with pens or paper clips while he was talking or shuffling papers around their desks.

"Your work sounds fascinating. And so rewarding, I would think," Victoria said and sounded genuinely interested. "My parents did some work with underprivileged kids all over the world. But that was long before I was born. I love hearing the stories."

Marco knew this was excellent intel she was giving him that he could use in getting her mother to give a donation to the foundation and he encouraged her to tell him more. "I would love to hear some of those stories."

Just then, Mrs. Van Hough stepped in and stopped the information gathering cold. "Yes. Yes, Mr. DeFranco. We would love to tell you more, but must move on. We have a few friends to see before we head home and it's getting late. Call my assistant next week and she can set up an appointment for you to come to the office and talk further," said Mrs. Van Hough as she held out a business card for Marco. With that, she stepped in front of her daughter and with the precision of a well-trained herding dog guided her away and down the ramp.

Conflicting emotions filled Marco as he watched them walk away. Victoria, huh? She was certainly beautiful, but smart, too. Marco didn't normally get to interact with women like her, and he was disappointed to have so little time to get to know her. But in the end, he knew his primary objective was to get donations for his foundation. In that regard, the meeting was a bit of a letdown. At least he got a commitment to meet with Mrs. Van Hough. Hopefully that would turn into a check.

He decided to remain on this floor for a while longer, then return to the main level to reconnect with Allison to see if she had anything to report before he left. "I wonder what they taste like..." Marco repeated as he laughed out loud. He took a seat on a bench behind him and waited as he enjoyed the abundance of good people-watching. He saw a man walk by and look at his wristwatch. For the price of the man's Rolex, Marco could have done a lot of good things. He looked down at his own wristwatch, which was an inexpensive TAG Heuer knockoff that he got last year. It still looked pretty good.

Twenty minutes passed. An enjoyable twenty minutes, Marco admitted, before he got back on his feet and headed down the ramp to the ground floor. He walked past the drink table, then the sushi tables, which were all being taken down. The night was almost over and the crowd had thinned out considerably. Marco reached the bottom of the ramp and was startled by a touch to his back. Firm, it beckoned him to turn around. When he did, he saw that Victoria was standing there in front of him.

"I'm afraid I don't have much time. My mother is intent on dragging me out of this place soon. But I wanted to tell you I really enjoyed hearing about your work and would love to hear more."

Running into her three times tonight was more than just a coincidence, and Marco knew he would regret it if he didn't take a chance to get to know her better. "I would love to. Maybe we can get some coffee sometime and talk some more."

Without hesitation, Victoria replied, "That would be great." Simultaneously, she reached inside Marco's breast pocket of his tuxedo and quickly snatched out his phone. It lit up, and she turned it to his face to unlock the screen. After she turned it back around, she entered a phone number into it and saved it in the phone's memory. She replaced it back in Marco's pocket and patted it to make sure it was still there. Finally, she turned to walk away, glancing back briefly at him one more time. As she walked toward the double doors to exit, he noticed that Mrs. Van Hough had witnessed everything. *She really does watch out for her daughter*, he thought, and for a minute, his heart sank. Did that mean he wouldn't be seeing Victoria again? And what about the check he was hoping to get from her mother? Only time would tell.

With the departure of his number one prospect, Marco was finally done for the night and with that acknowledgment, a wave of relief and fatigue set in. He scanned the room looking for Allison and found her standing near the coat-check stand. He began the slow, painful walk to where she was standing. Painful not because anything physically hurt, but his ego was a little bruised. He had been sure they would leave with money tonight. Instead, he would have to tell her he struck out. But he reassured himself that it was not all bad. After all, he'd gotten an appointment with Mrs. Van Hough for next week. That was definitely progress.

As he got closer to her, he noticed that she had a broad smile on her face. Allison was normally an upbeat person, but this smile was big even by her standards. He picked up the pace and closed the distance between them quickly. He couldn't wait to hear what had gotten her so excited, and wondered if she had a promising lead.

"What has got you so darn giddy?" Marco said even before he came to a stop in front of her.

"Way to use that sex appeal, Marco. You have done a lot of things to get money from donors, but I think this is a first. The Van Houghs' daughter? Nice play."

Marco was totally oblivious to the implications she was making. He was confused, tired, and his brain wasn't firing quite right. "I'm not getting you. Spell it out for me, Allison."

"You hit on the daughter to get to the mom's money. Genius. Make the pitch to her and let her go back to mommy for the money. I'm impressed."

It finally registered with Marco. "No. That's not at all what happened. She was interested in hearing more about the foundation. It was her idea, not mine."

"Does that mean it's a date? Is *the* Marco DeFranco going on an actual date?" she asked with a sound in her voice that was a cross between amazement and jealousy. In the nearly five years since working for the foundation, Allison had never seen or heard of Marco ever dating anyone. She thought it was strange for such a good-looking guy to have no interest in intimacy, but he was swamped trying to stay employed and run the foundation.

"I'm not even sure I'll call her. And if I do, it will be business only, I assure you."

"Well, Marco, can I tell you something purely from a woman's perspective?"

Marco blurted back, "You're going to whether or not I want to hear it."

Allison frowned and then continued, "You're probably right. Listen, that woman is really into you. You need to be careful around her."

Again, Marco was confused. *I need to go home and go to bed. This has not been my best night*, he thought to himself. "Into me in what way? I don't understand," he continued.

"I watched the way she approached you and how she gave you her number. Trust me, women know these things."

"Allison, listen. In case you didn't realize it, Victoria Van Hough comes from money. Lots of money. And I don't. That never works."

"I'm not discounting that, but she is obviously interested in you. I mean romantically."

Marco snorted loudly at the thought. "Go home, Allison. I think the martinis are getting to you. Send me an email in the morning with anything you managed to uncover tonight. Besides this fictional romance you are brewing in your head. Good night." And with that, he turned and headed to the exit.

"Don't be so quick to dismiss what I told you. I know what I saw!" Allison yelled as Marco walked away.

I'm losing my mind, I swear, Marco said to himself as he exited the aquarium, walking down the sidewalk toward the limo. And with that, he swept any thoughts of Victoria out of his mind. For now.

CHAPTER FOUR
Marco

The brakes on the limo squeaked as it came to a stop where Marco instructed the driver to do so. "Are you sure this is where you want to go, Mr. DeFranco?" said the driver with an air of concern. "Yes. It's fine. I know this neighborhood well." He thanked the driver as he exited the limo and stepped to the curb. The limo pulled away, leaving Marco alone with only his thoughts of the night at the aquarium. Marco looked out of place dressed in his tuxedo. The neighborhood comprised old, run-down, abandoned buildings intermixed with single-wide mobile homes and vacant lots. The evidence of gang activity was painted everywhere. It was dark and dangerous, but Marco knew it well. He knew that a man in a tuxedo at this time of night might attract unwanted "friends" so he moved down the road with a sense of purpose.

He reached the corner and turned left down a cul-de-sac. Numerous dogs broke out into barking fits as he walked past their homes. At the end of the block was a chain-link fence, and behind it an abandoned warehouse. The building caught fire several years ago and now stood, or partially stood, unchanged. It was a magnet for death and destruction. Just before getting to the gate leading to the warehouse, Marco made a right and went up a gravel driveway. As he walked, motion-sensing lights popped on, illuminating his way. At the end, the last two lights came on, and Marco's destination became clear. It was a 1979 Winnebago travel trailer, white with gold stripes and in surprisingly excellent condition given its advanced age. The windows were all intact and covered by curtains. There weren't any lights visible inside the trailer, and no signs of activity. Marco went up the two stairs leading to the front door. He looked around to make sure he was alone, then slipped a key in the lock and opened the door. Marco stepped into the trailer, flipped on the light switch, and closed the door behind him, ensuring the lock was fully seated in the doorframe. This wasn't a place where you wanted to leave your door unlocked.

The light from the fixture chased away much of the darkness and revealed a relatively intact, well-maintained home. Marco's home. He had lived here for the past five years. To the right, there was a small sofa. Straight ahead was the booth where he ate, dreamed, planned, and worked. To the left was the kitchen and small bathroom, and at the end was Marco's bedroom. His total living space was about 150 square feet. Small, but plenty for him. In a sense, his house was a perfect representation of his life: sensible, financially responsible, livable. Although safe was probably not a word he would have put on that list. He wished he could have, but these were the people he served, and he wanted to live among them. Otherwise, how would he have understood their concerns or needs? Besides, it was all he could afford. Marco put every penny he got in donations, and most of his salary as a social worker, into his foundation. Admittedly, it was an unconventional living situation, but it was him.

Marco took his patent leather shoes off and stowed them in a nearby closet. He went back to the bedroom and removed his tuxedo. Carefully he put it back into the protective cover and hung it in the closet. Marco was meticulous in how he put things away. *Everything has a place and everything in its place*, he thought.

Marco trekked the five steps from his bedroom to the bathroom and took a well-deserved shower. As the scalding water ran over his exhausted body, he replayed the events of the evening. All things considered, he was pleased. He had already put an appointment in his calendar to call Mrs. Van Hough on Wednesday morning. Hopefully, he could get in to see her before the end of the week. He learned some extremely useful information tonight that he might have been able to use to leverage a nice check from her.

After drying off, he put on a pair of shorts, got a bottle of water from the refrigerator, and moved to the booth. This was his office as well, and he did most of his work here. He opened up his laptop and pressed the Start button. While it booted up, Marco looked around the room and noticed the calendar he had hung on a nail in the wall. He leaned forward and took it down to scrutinize it. He did this regularly and had for many years. Each page of the calendar had a picture of the latest model of Airstream travel trailers. The trailers represented freedom, and freedom meant that Marco could easily take his foundation on the road to California. There was a tremendous need for his services in Los Angeles, and he yearned to be there helping. His trailer would allow him to, once again, live and serve directly in the community. He never thought about it before, but the chrome appearance of the trailers reminded him of a bullet. His silver bullet. Marco closed his eyes, and a picture appeared in his mind. Marco was standing next to his dad in front of an Airstream. He smiled and opened them up again. The calendar reminded Marco of his dad, too. He remembered the good times he had with him and their trailer.

He flipped the pages backward. January had a Nest model. "Cute, but way too small. Even for me." March was the Classic model. This was their flagship trailer. Big and beautiful. But way out of his price range. He made his way to September, admiring each one as he went. "There it is." The page was dog-eared and worn. More so than any of the other pages. "The Flying Cloud. Perfect." He loved the classic lines and the shiny exterior. So distinctive and instantly recognizable. He would be sad to see October 1 come since he had to move on from this model. He would definitely get one. Soon. It was what drove him. He thought, *My passions: the foundation and my Airstream.*

He put the calendar down and glanced at his cell phone. It turned on when he picked it up, and it unlocked when it recognized his face. Marco saw that his contacts app was open. He always closed all his apps to conserve battery life, so this was unexpected. Just as he swiped up to close the app, something caught his eye. A new entry. He looked more closely and saw the entry was titled *VVH* and there was a new phone number. *VVH.* Victoria Van Hough. He completely forgot about that. He imagined the possibilities. If he could convince Victoria of the value of a contribution to his foundation, she might have convinced her mom. Marco was confident in his ability to convince Mrs. Van Hough, but he would not have turned away any extra help. *Why not improve my odds?* He thought back to his conversation with Allison and her insistence that he had a plan to use Victoria. *She gave me way too much credit.* He laughed out loud. But it was actually a good idea. What he didn't agree with was Allison's insistence that Victoria was interested in a romantic relationship. How could she possibly have known that? He discounted that notion out of hand. He looked around at his house and imagined the mansion that she probably lived in. *Sure. She can just move right in.* Regardless, it took two to start a relationship, and he was not in the market at this time.

He called up her contact information, unfamiliar with any social protocols regarding getting cups of coffee and talking business. He planned a simple text. *Hi Victoria. It's Marco. It was nice meeting you tonight. I'm available next weekend for coffee if you are. Please look at your schedule and let me know.*

Marco was unsure of this text but hit Send. It was late, so he assumed he might get a response tomorrow. He put his phone down, rehung the calendar on the nail, and closed his laptop. He was way too tired to work anymore tonight.

His phone came to life and barked out, "Show me the money!" Marco jumped with surprise. He loved that text notification sound. Not terribly professional though. "That was fast," he remarked as he picked his phone back up. The text read, *I'm so glad to hear from you, Marco! I'd love to have coffee with you! Let me look at my schedule, and I'll get back to you in a day or two. Have a great night!* She ended it with several emojis.

"Seems like an excessive number of exclamation points," Marco remarked. But he didn't care. Success! He put a reminder in his phone to get back in touch with her by Wednesday in case she didn't get back to him. He wouldn't need it. Not by a long shot.

CHAPTER FIVE
Victoria

I look great, Victoria said to herself as she checked out her makeup in the mirror. She sucked her lips together to distribute the ruby red lipstick across them, then made a kissing face at herself. "Perfect." The traffic light turned green, and she closed the mirror and folded her visor back into the up position. She accelerated through the intersection and down the street. Victoria replayed the events in her mind of what got her to this point, and it made her happy. She saw Marco at the fundraising event exactly one week ago and was immediately attracted to him. He was tall, she guessed just over six feet, thin, but not too thin with dark brown hair, deep brown eyes, and age appropriate. And he was extremely handsome. All those physical features were just icing on the Marco cake to Victoria, because she was most impressed with his confidence and how he conducted himself. He spoke intelligently and seemed to really have his life together. *I bet he's a good kisser*, she thought, and allowed her mind to drift to other possibilities.

When she first met Marco, she had a great feeling, but doors of opportunity close quickly so she had to act. It wasn't easy though. Her mother saw the look in Victoria's eyes when she met Marco and lectured her for several minutes about finding an appropriate young man. "He's not one of us, Victoria dear. Don't even think about it," was her mother's position. "He'll take you for your money... actually *my* money. Then he'll leave you. You have to trust me on that." Her mother looked her in the eyes in a stern, motherly way when she made that last point. But Victoria was not listening. At thirty-two years old, she had to admit that she sometimes still acted like an impulsive teenager.

When the chance to get to know Marco further presented itself, she pounced. There he was, at the bottom of the ramp, and her mother was all the way over by the door. Perfect timing, so she took the chance. She laughed to herself as she circled the block, looking for a place to park her Mercedes. She was not sure what came over her when she reached in his pocket and took out his cell phone. She knew it was there because she saw him place it there earlier. Victoria wanted him to know she was an assertive woman who went after the things she wanted in life. *Mission accomplished on that one sister*, she said to herself. She realized that there was a fine line between being assertive and leaving the man feeling emasculated. *I hope I didn't go too far*, she thought as she parallel parked her car near the coffee shop.

She'd been pleasantly surprised when Marco had texted her so quickly. Victoria took that as a sign of his powerful interest in getting to know her. She'd told him she had to check her schedule, but there was nothing that would keep her from this first meeting. She'd texted him back Monday morning, and the date was set. Since then, they had texted a few times, sharing some basic information about each other, but nothing deep. Victoria thought it was so cute that he emailed her some information about his foundation. Of course she was interested in that and his life in general. However, it was so darling how he used that as a pretense to get her out for coffee. She would have gone regardless.

She closed the car door and glanced at herself in the side mirror. "Fabulous," she said, and by most measures, she was. Dressed in a formfitting red dress with matching earrings and a necklace as well as her favorite pair of designer shoes, she enjoyed how she looked. She pulled her dress down to smooth out the wrinkles and covered the fifty yards between her and the front door to the coffee shop. Just inside the door, she saw Marco and her face lit up. He stood and opened the door for her. "Hi, Marco! Nice to see you again," she said and moved in to give him a hug and a light kiss on the cheek. She was a touchy-feely person and enjoyed physical contact. As they embraced, she took in a lungful of his wonderful scent. It was clean and sophisticated.

"Thanks for coming," Marco said and extended his hand to direct her to the table where they would meet. They walked down the aisle and he invited her to sit down at the booth while he sat across from her. *Just like I remembered him*, she thought. *Good-looking.*

After settling in, the server came by and took their order. "Coffee, black," Victoria ordered. She hated café coffee. Actually, she hated most coffee in the United States. At home, she drank Colombian coffee imported by the family business. *It's not like the garbage we drink here*, she thought, but she would suffer through it. Totally worth it. Marco ordered only water with lemon. Victoria wondered what that said about Marco. Frugal? Health conscious? She settled on "practical."

Marco looked across the table at her with those big brown eyes and she got a little lost in them. "Did you hear me?" he asked.

"Sorry, it's a little loud in here. I didn't," she said, knowing it was a lie. And what a gentleman he was, letting her get away with it.

"No problem. I asked if you got my email with the information about my foundation," he inquired.

"I sure did, but before we get into that, tell me about yourself. Tell me about your family and growing up," she said as she choked down a sip of the worst cup of coffee she had ever had.

He seemed to hesitate a little and took a minute or two to gather his thoughts, but Victoria waited patiently. She had learned to not just jump in and fill the silence. Marco took a drink of his water then started, "Well, I had a pretty typical upbringing. I grew up on the far western side of the city in a middle-class neighborhood with my two brothers and one sister. My parents owned a family bakery, and we all worked there in the morning and all summer. That experience really taught me a solid work ethic that I carry to my foundation today."

Victoria sensed that he was a little hesitant to discuss his background, but she chalked it up to nerves. "Where did you go to college?" she said, trying to redirect the conversation.

"I went to Parkland College and got an associate degree in psychology."

"Nice. Do you think you could psychoanalyze me?" Victoria said playfully. "Hypnotize me? Perform exposure therapy on me?" Victoria was proud of her play on words and repeated it again in her head, *exposure therapy*. She smiled, and he seemed to enjoy her playfulness. Marco let out a laugh, and a smirk formed on his face.

"Sorry," she apologized and batted her big blue eyes at him. "Tell me about after college. You aren't working for the family bakery anymore?"

"No. I'm not. My father passed away when I was younger, and my family moved to the suburbs. My older brothers took over the bakery. We really didn't get along, but that wasn't the reason. I felt extremely unfulfilled. I wasn't doing a job that made me feel good about myself."

"Making donuts wasn't cutting it for you, huh?" she asked, then noticed, as she shifted her weight in her seat, that his feet were on her side, under the table. Their legs were touching, but she didn't move hers. She enjoyed the contact.

"No. I moved back to the city and started my foundation. I really have a desire to help people. But not just any people, we're talking the most vulnerable ones in society. Imagine having literally nothing. No place to live, no family, no social support. Nothing. You're not even sure where your next meal will come from. These are the ones I target. I see a lot of women with children who are victims of domestic violence. I help people with severe mental health issues. Men who have been cast out of society, especially poor men with HIV."

Victoria listened intently. She was genuinely impressed with the passion he brought to his work. As he talked, she imagined him bringing that kind of passion into a relationship and she felt more attracted to him. He was a good man. He would be a good catch. But as he talked, Victoria found that her mind was wandering from the conversation. She was more interested in him as a person and not as a business executive. As time passed, she found herself nodding and saying things like "I see" and "Interesting, please tell me more."

"I printed out some documents I call bio-sheets. They tell the story of a few of the success stories from my foundation. Each sheet focuses on a different person or family unit." Marco opened a file folder on the table and pulled out three individual sheets. Victoria scanned each page as he turned them toward her. Their hands casually touched as he slid each one across the table. *He has soft hands*, she noted. Each sheet that was passed was like a glossy brochure. A nice full-color picture of a person was at the top of each sheet, below the name of his foundation. First, a woman with her child smiled in front of a cute small house. Second, a military veteran with two prosthetic legs and one arm. The third sheet featured a young man in front of a pizza oven. Each sheet told the story of the person at the top. Victoria was impressed. They were high quality and well done. They spoke to the success of his foundation.

"These are excellent, Marco, but I really need to see more," Victoria said as she worked toward her hidden agenda. She wanted more time to get to know Marco, and he seemed intent on continuing his sales pitch. *It feels like we are role-playing,* she thought. *Who doesn't like a good role-playing exercise?* and a small grin came over her face that she quickly wiped away.

"I have literally dozens of them I can email you," Marco responded, appearing to be somewhat in tune with her actual intent. But he continued to stay the course.

"No, Marco. What I mean is, I have to see your foundation more closely. It needs to be more exposed to me," Victoria said, wondering if her playfulness had crossed the line with him. "I need to see you in action."

Marco hesitated.

"Okay. I can do that." He pulled his phone out of his pocket and opened up his calendar. "Let me take a look. How about next Saturday? I can show you around and you can see the outstanding work the foundation does."

"Then it's a date!" she said, and the smile on his face told her he felt the same way. "Text me the details and I'll be there."

Brimming with confidence, she pushed the half-full cup of coffee away and stood up to leave. Marco seemed confused, as if surprised by her abrupt departure but stood up, too. "Oh, okay," he said as she dragged him in for another hug and another chance to catch his wonderful scent. She was pleasantly surprised when he hugged her back and held her tight. She thanked him again, turned and walked to the door. She hoped he was watching her as she left. She slipped into her car, closed the door, and took a deep breath. She could still smell his scent and couldn't wait to see him again. Victoria started the car and pulled away, imagining their next time together.

CHAPTER SIX
Marco

After two-and-a-half hours of staring at his laptop screen, Marco needed to take a break. He saved his work, rubbed his eyes, and closed the laptop. He had been working long hours at his day job, leaving precious little time at night to keep the foundation going. Without his efforts, the funds would have dried up and it would have been game over. But the more he got in donations, the more he spent on the community. It was the way he liked it. He retrieved a bottle of water from the refrigerator and plopped back down in the booth. He should have hired more help, but he couldn't convince himself to pull the trigger. Besides, his plan was to purchase his Airstream and head to California as soon as humanly, and more importantly, financially possible. The thought brought a slight pain to him when he thought about Allison and him cutting ties. After all, she had worked for him for a few years. *Has it been two years? Three?* he wondered, but couldn't remember. *No worries, she always reminds me whenever the day rolls around,* he acknowledged.

He checked his watch and realized it was 9:45. Just a few more minutes, he thought, as he opened up his laptop again. As he did, he noticed a faint light shining through the front window shade next to the door. It was just a sliver, but it let him know someone was walking down the driveway. The light got brighter and brighter as more of the motion-sensing lights outside were activated until the last two by the front door came to life. At that point, the sliver went around both sides and the bottom of the window shade. It was a kind of guard dog for him. He counted, "One, two..." and when he said, "Three," the door opened and in walked Allison.

"Hi, Allison. Sorry for asking you to stop by so late, but we really need to get these documents finished tomorrow, and I had no way to get them to you."

"No worries at all," she responded as Marco fanned through several file folders before he plucked one out of the stack and handed it to her.

"By the way, I forgot to ask, how did your coffee go with Victoria the other day? You make any progress on a donation from her mom?" Allison didn't normally ask about his personal life, but she could use the cover of something that was business related. Besides, last time they discussed it, Marco still insisted there were no romantic intentions from either party. It was strictly business.

"Honestly, it was a little weird," he said, closing the laptop again.

"How so?" she asked, her curiosity starting to build.

"Well, for starters, she wanted to know about my background."

"Marco, not that I want to defend her because, as you know, I think she wants more out of you, but what's so weird about that? A lot of donors want to know your background. That makes them feel comfortable giving you money."

"No, no. She asked about my childhood and growing up. About my family and the family business," Marco continued.

Allison fought the formation of an enormous smile on her face as she asked, "Anything else?"

Marco thought for a minute and replied, "She insisted on hugging me and said something like 'I'm a touchy person.'"

"OMG," Allison said, using texting shorthand in verbal communication, which always annoyed Marco. But she was only twenty-five, so he forgave her for adolescent things like that. Allison's smile was impossible to miss now. "Anything else?" she asked, barely able to get the words out of her mouth.

"Yeah. Towards the end, she said she needed to see me in action and I should expose more to her," Marco finished.

Allison couldn't control herself anymore. She burst out into laughter so loud, it startled Marco. She put her hand over her mouth and tried to stifle it, but that only made it worse. As she laughed, she crossed her arms over her abdomen and bent at the waist. When she stood up again, her face was red, and a tear ran down her face.

After she caught her breath and wiped away the tear, she continued, "Marco, come on now," her words interrupted by random bursts of laughter. "I've known you for almost five years. You can't possibly think this woman is only interested in a business transaction."

Marco got up from the table and Allison knew she had struck a nerve with him. "Allison, I'm tired and going to bed. Lock the door on your way out."

As he walked back to the bedroom and closed the door, he still heard her trying to stifle her laughter as she left. He got undressed and slipped under the covers. Before he could consider any of the things that Allison said to him, Marco fell fast asleep.

***

As his subconscious mind gave way to his conscious one, he heard a sound. It was faint. *Beep, beep, beep.* Marco rolled over, opened his eyes, and decided that he felt like crap. He hadn't been sleeping well for the past week or so. "I'm sure it's the pressure I'm feeling," he said to himself.

Beep, beep, beep.

He thought about taking some time off and tried to remember when he had gone on any kind of vacation last. He knew the answer: never.

Beep, beep, beep.

What the hell was that noise? he thought. Then it dawned on him. His cell phone. The noise was the alarm he used on his phone. He was late! Again!

He jumped out of bed, opened the door, and dove into the booth to shut his phone off. He realized that in his rush to get away from Allison the Interrogator and her white-hot light of truth, he had left his phone sitting on the table. "Damn it." He retrieved his phone and headed back to the bedroom to get ready for work. "No time to shower today," he concluded after checking the time. As he dressed, he thought back to his conversation with Allison. It made him a little mad. She hadn't been there. How the hell did she know anyone's intentions? Being a fair man, he briefly considered her perspective, and how she would have interpreted Victoria's actions if she had been there instead. *Is it possible? Is Allison right?* he mused as he hurriedly got dressed. Maybe? But he concluded that it still didn't matter. She was the daughter of an incredibly important potential client. He closed the front door and locked it, thinking, *I don't poop where I eat... I don't poop in my own nest... I don't dip my pen in the company ink.* And with each saying, he laughed harder.

CHAPTER SEVEN
Marco

The train slowed as it approached the next stop. This was where he got off, so he started collecting the boxes he brought with him. Two in each hand. The door opened, and he stepped onto the platform, making his way around the ticket booth and over to the pickup area. He saw his ride waiting patiently for him. Marco opened the rear door and gently placed his packages on the seat. He closed the door and moved to the passenger-side door, opened it and sat down. Within seconds Marco's oldest brother, Sal, was on him. His huge hands were all over the top of Marco's head, tousling his hair. "There's my baby brother!" he said as he fought with Marco to continue this annoying tradition. Marco deflected some of this assault, then his brother moved to the hitting phase. He gently punched him in the arm and leg that were exposed to him. Marco let it play out and it finally stopped. He knew better than to protest. It wouldn't have mattered. His brother had greeted him like this for years. "I sure miss you, baby brother," he said again as the two men composed themselves. He put the car in drive and pulled away from the curb.

"I'm not ten years old anymore, Sal," Marco said, sounding somewhat annoyed as the car began the fifteen-minute trip to their family home.

"Glad you could make it," Sal said. "It's great to see you."

"Did I have a choice?" Marco asked, already knowing the answer.

"If you enjoy breaking Mom's heart, you do," snorted Sal. Marco knew this was true. He came from a deeply traditional Italian family. His parents emigrated from Central Italy before having kids. They settled in the city and stayed there until his dad passed away. Sunday dinners were an expected part of being in this family. They started out every Sunday. Then they moved to every other Sunday. Now, years later, given that all the kids were grown up and had kids of their own, the family dinner only happened once a month. Marco's mom wasn't happy about this, but tried to understand they all had their own lives. But Sal was right. If Marco hadn't shown up, it would have broken his mom's heart. He was the baby, after all. Her baby.

Lucky for Marco, Sal wasn't in a talkative mood, so they rode along in silence. Marco wasn't very fond of these monthly dinners. It wasn't the inconvenience of having to come from the city. It was an easy thirty-five-minute train ride. The problem was that every time they got together, the conversation turned to Marco, and the questions flowed. "Marco, when are you going to get a girlfriend?" "Marco, when are you going to have kids?" "Marco, why don't you move back to the suburbs?" And many others. They all knew the answers. *When I move to California, things will be different*, he thought to himself. That part of the plan, they didn't know.

The car came to a stop in the street across from the house. Sal got out with Marco, and Marco gathered the boxes in the back seat. Sal held his hand out and offered to take some of them, so Marco handed him two.

"Be careful," Marco implored, but Sal waved his concerns away with one hand as he carelessly slung the boxes around with the other.

They walked down the driveway and headed for the back door to enter the kitchen. It was not quite a perp walk for Marco, but close.

As he approached, he could already smell the food. It was strong, and the garlic slapped him in the face. He loved it. It reminded him of growing up. The better days, anyway. As he stepped into the kitchen, he heard it.

"My little pasticcino!!!" exclaimed Marco's mom.

"Hi, Ma," Marco replied as she collected him up into her waiting arms. She hugged him hard and held him there.

"Look what I brought," Sal said to his mom, holding up the two boxes he had carried for Marco.

"Salvatore, you put those down. I know who brought them!" Mom admonished Sal. The boxes skidded across the counter as Sal carelessly plopped them down and walked into the next room. With her arms still firmly locked around Marco, she whispered in his ear, "Are those the cannolis?"

"Of course they are. Plus some other goodies I made," Marco whispered back.

"Oh, pasticcino!" she repeated, calling him the nickname he had since he was a child. *Cupcake.* How he wished that name would have just died. She lightened her grip on him so she could look at him face-to-face. "You were always the best baker in the family... except your father, God rest his soul. Won't you come back to the bakery and work with your brothers? Make your mamma happy," Mom said, laying it on Marco with a thick layer of guilt.

That didn't take long, Marco thought. "You know the answer to that, Ma," Marco replied softly, trying hard to keep his mom's heart intact.

"You can't blame your mom for trying," she said as she released her grip on Marco. "But I still love you." She planted a sweet kiss on his cheek.

Marco looked around the kitchen. The heat was oppressive. All the windows were open, as was the door, with no effect on the temperature. Every burner on the stove was in use with pots in full boil. The oven light was on and baking dishes were inside. The sink was already overflowing with dirty dishes. It was obvious Mom had been cooking all day. No surprise. A small plate sat on the counter next to the stove with a nice selection of items: prosciutto, cheese, bread, tomatoes, and olive oil. Mom picked up the plate and handed it to Marco. "Mangia, mangia!" she said, encouraging him to eat. "You're too thin, Marco!" He took the plate and began to eat. He hated to disappoint his mom. "How are you doing, Marco?" she inquired.

"I'm fine, Mamma. Just really busy with work and the foundation," Marco responded as he shoveled the food into his mouth. He wouldn't have lied. Food wasn't always plentiful at his house. It took time to shop and cook, which wasn't a part of his life plan. And he loved his mom's cooking.

"Now go say hi to your family," said Mom. Marco set the empty plate down, returned a kiss to his mom's cheek, and headed toward the living room.

As he emerged from the hallway, he saw a common sight. The same sight he saw every month. People were everywhere. Vinny, the middle brother, was sitting on the couch with his wife. Val, his only sister, was there, too, along with Sal, their respective spouses and half a dozen children who ran around wildly. *What a zoo*, Marco thought to himself.

"Uncle Marco!!" came a chorus of little voices as they surrounded Marco and began pulling on his legs. The children ranged in age from eight down to a year old. Most were mobile and currently engaged in trying to pull him to the ground. Marco feigned a loss of control and fell to the ground while five children piled on top of him. He rolled over and tried to tickle as many of them as he could as they all ran away and hid. While on his knees, Marco greeted each of the adults in the room. In succession, each of the children returned individually from their hiding spots and dove at Marco. He loved playing with them as much as they loved playing with Marco.

After about forty minutes of play, Mom called out to the wives for help in the kitchen. One by one, they carried dishes full of food to the dining room table. So many dishes. So much food. Marco shook his head as they piled up. It was a challenge to move some other dishes around to make room for new ones. Mom made braciola, pasta fazool, and risotto, among other classic Italian dishes. *She's feeding an army*, Marco thought. *What I could do with all this food.* Once the table was set, dishes were served for the kids and they were seated at the kids' table to eat. As this proceeded, the other adults worked their way into the dining room and took their seats. Always the same. Everyone sat in the same spot every month. As the oldest male, Sal sat at the head of the table where his father would have sat. He missed his father so much. *Maybe this is why I don't enjoy coming here*, he wondered. Mom sat to Sal's right in a chair with the easiest access to the kitchen, and everyone else took their usual seats. Everyone bowed their heads and Sal asked the blessing after which everyone said, "Amen," then "Buon appetito!"

Marco was thankful for this part of the day. Everyone was so busy filling their mouths with delicious food, they were too occupied to turn their focus to Marco. But as the ravaged hoard depleted the piles of food, the silence soon ended.

"So Marco, how is work going? The 'foundation' doing okay?" Vinny started the attack off in a seemingly inoffensive way, but used his fingers to form air quotes when he said foundation. This was his way of expressing contempt for it. Some of those at the adult table smirked. They knew it was starting, and they enjoyed their front row seats.

"Vinny. Why do you always have to start with me? Mom, tell him to stop," Marco replied insistently.

"Vinny, stop. Leave your brother alone. He can do what he wants with his life," Mom protested, but only half-heartedly. She would have loved for Marco to finally give in, move back to the suburbs and come work for the family bakery.

"No, seriously. When are you going to realize that you are only one person? You can't save the world," Vinny continued.

"You don't understand what I do. I've changed the lives of dozens of people," Marco said, trying to defend himself.

Val chimed in, which was unexpected, since she normally said nothing. "Marco, you live in a trailer in the city. I just feel so sorry for you."

Marco replied sharply, "I feel sorry for all of you! Do you know what it's like to do something you love? To change someone's life?" His blood pressure was rising, and he desperately wanted to change the subject. "How's the bakery?"

"It's doing well, but could use your help, Marco," Mom said without realizing that she was just adding fuel to the family fire. "It's growing so much that the boys have to work long hours to keep up."

"Then they should hire someone else to help," Marco responded.

"Marco!" Mom said, almost gasping. "Oh, mio Dio. What would your father think if he heard you suggesting that someone outside the family help run the bakery? Your father worked so hard to build that business." She looked toward the sky when she talked about her late husband.

In an attempt to change the subject from this uncomfortable topic, Sal asked, "Are you still dating that girl?"

This question caught Marco by surprise. It hadn't been asked for a while, and it caused him to think back to last year. He recalled being so tired of everyone asking him when he would find a girlfriend that he did something he would forever regret. In a moment of desperation, he asked Allison to go with him to the monthly family dinner. If they saw him with a woman, they might get off his back. That was his hope, but it blew up in his face. His family fell in love with Allison. She was so outgoing and personable. Allison fell in love with them as well. She didn't have a family and really took to them. It all happened so fast. They were so excited that Marco had finally found someone. And Allison, somehow, got the impression that they were going beyond just a working relationship. Marco was sure he had explained to her the purpose of bringing her there. He'd needed to get his family off his back. But she'd taken it differently. Her feelings had been hurt, and it took a long time to repair the relationship. Fortunately, they had patched things up, but the family still asked about her from time to time.

"I told you before, that she works for me. We aren't dating. We will never date," Marco replied.

"You should date her. She is totally into you," commented Val.

What is with women? How does she know? Marco thought. "She's perfectly satisfied with her job as my assistant."

"And she's a real looker, brother," Vinny said with a wink to Marco, which brought a laugh to the table.

"Not gonna happen. End of story," Marco said as he got up and went to the kitchen. He busied himself by opening the boxes he brought. Two boxes were full of cookies and cakes. Two were full of cannolis. All baked by Marco. He was an excellent baker, but damn it, he didn't want to work with his brothers. They sucked the life out of him. Besides, he was doing what he wanted. It was his "calling." He wasn't overly religious, but he liked that word. Unfortunately, he knew the lack of spiritual direction in his life would have disappointed his mom, but he only had so much time in the day. He thought she should get in line behind all the others who were disappointed in him. Just then she came into the kitchen.

"Let me help you, patatino," his mom said in her most soothing voice.

"Mom, that makes no sense. Little potato?" Marco shot

back, still annoyed from the dinner conversation.

"It means love. Don't ask me, honey. I didn't invent the language. I just speak it." They took the pastries out of the boxes and placed them on serving trays. As they worked, Mom asked, "Are you coming for dinner next month?"

Marco had been dreading this topic and hoped it would not come up today. After hesitating, he asked, "Why did you plan it for that weekend? That's six weeks away."

"I'm sorry patatino. It was the only weekend your brothers and sister could do it."

He continued to work, only looking at her out of the corner of his eye. "Mom, you know that's the date of the biggest fundraiser of the year. My foundation really needs the money and I have to be there. I have a chance to get a large donation from someone. I've been working on this for a long time and it would really change the things I can do in the community."

His mom lowered her head, and disappointment spread over her face. "Oh, Marco..." Mom's voice trailed off in a combination of hurt feelings and manipulation.

"Besides, everyone will have a better time without me here. Listen to them!" he implored as the sound of voices could be heard behind them, all debating the best way for Marco to close his foundation and move back to the suburbs.

"They mean well and love you, too, Marco," Mom stated as she looked up from the pastries and into his eyes.

"They are rude and condescending and if they loved me, they would accept me and the choices I have made for my life," Marco spouted back, immediately regretting the tone of voice he had taken with his mom.

Mom looked at Marco and frowned. "When I'm gone, they are all you will have left. Please don't push them away."

They took the serving trays into the dining room, where the family had continued to debate Marco's life choices. He listened to his mom's words, and they stuck with him. He sat quietly as they went back and forth about the direction

Marco should take.

"He needs to get out of that terrible trailer and move back here. He could find a sweet woman and settle down," said Vinny's wife, Marge.

Val added, "I have so many friends who would be great with him!" She looked over at Marco and said, "Please?" Marco stuffed a cannoli into his mouth to keep from saying what he wanted to say to her.

After forty-five minutes, the family had solved all of Marco's problems. He was moving to the suburbs ("There is a great house about three blocks from here," Marge suggested), he was working at the bakery (Sal was going to put his exceptional baking skills to good use), and Val had the perfect woman for him. He would have three kids within the next five years. Marco barely listened as he continued to eat the pastries he made. *They are right about one thing*, he admitted to himself. *I am a great baker.*

CHAPTER EIGHT
Marco

Marco rounded the corner and headed east down 14th Street, past beauty shops, bars, and restaurants. This was an area of the city where "Mom and Pop" were well represented. Traffic was light at many of the restaurants since this was the time between late lunch and early dinner. Soon enough, they would be packed with customers.

It was a beautiful fall day and Marco was enjoying the 1.5-mile walk from his home to the rendezvous point he chose for his meeting with Victoria. Occasionally, he wished he owned a car, but today, he was enjoying the fresh air and solitude. As he walked, Marco reflected on his meeting with Victoria. The meeting felt strange to Marco, but he couldn't put his finger on why. His preparation had been excellent. As he usually did, he'd sent pre-meeting information to his prospect for her review. He had also included some of his most impressive bio-sheets from his biggest success stories. He had arrived early, selected an appropriate setting, and came prepared with professionally printed information. But he couldn't figure out where he went wrong. He thought back to the beginning of the meeting and how Victoria had seemed more interested in him as a person than Marco as the head of the foundation. After he'd answered the unnecessary personal questions, he'd finally gotten into information about his foundation. But he had kept getting the feeling that Victoria was tuning him out. She had been nodding her head, but he didn't feel like she was listening. She had been staring into his eyes, and that made him uncomfortable. Marco thought back to Allison's comments that Victoria was really interested in a romantic relationship, but after a week had passed, he still didn't see it. When he'd felt like the day had been a total loss, Victoria had made a startling statement. She had wanted to see more. Maybe, he wondered, all wasn't lost. He thought back. "What did she say?" he said out loud as he walked. "She wanted me to expose my foundation to her. She wants to see more of me, and me in action," he said. Marco thought if seeing him in action was what she wanted, then that was exactly what she would get.

He took a position where he could see traffic approaching, so he knew when she arrived. Marco remembered her gray Mercedes, a two-door convertible. As always, he had a plan for a memorable day with his prospect. A day that would show his hard work and the impact his foundation had on the lives of others. He felt confident that after today, he would have a powerful ally to help in his effort to get a big donation from her mom. So far, he had had one meeting with Mrs. Van Hough, but didn't seem to make any progress with her. Victoria was just the help he needed.

Marco was surprised when Victoria emerged from a red Audi instead of her Mercedes and reminded himself that her mother drove a Bentley. He wondered how much money it took to maintain such a stable of expensive cars. He noticed that Victoria was dressed in a red, knee-length dress with white trim. Allison would say it was a designer dress with high-end shoes and an expensive handbag, an ensemble that cost what most people made in a month. She smoothed out her dress and crossed the street. When she saw him, Marco noticed how big she smiled. She picked up her pace and her arms opened long before she got to him. He braced himself for what was the inevitable hug coming his way.

"Hi, Marco!" she exclaimed as her arms scooped him up and held him close. Her long blond hair fell across his face as she seemed to squeeze him as tight as she could. She loosened up her grip and planted a kiss on his cheek. "It's really nice to see you again," she said.

"Nice to see you again, too," Marco replied, and noted that the hug and kiss weren't unpleasant. Just not typical for potential business associates, but he went with it.

"I can't wait to get started. What do you have planned for us?" Victoria asked with a Christmas-like excitement in her voice.

"I'm going to show you a world you never knew existed. Most people only get to see my bio-sheets and have to imagine what it's like for the people my foundation helps. You are going to get to meet some of them and see my work firsthand." This was the pitch Marco worked on last night, and he thought it played well with her. "But we have to do something first. Do you trust me?"

Victoria had a quizzical look on her face, but replied, "Of course I do, silly."

Victoria didn't know it, but in these first few minutes, Marco had to do some fast thinking because he realized a flaw in his original plan. "We have to go shopping," he said as he pulled out his phone and sent off a quick text.

"I love to shop. Who are we shopping for? Where is your car? Do you want me to drive?" Victoria fired off a series of questions before Marco could answer any of them.

"We'll walk," Marco said and pointed in the direction they would head. "Let your education begin."

They moved down the street together. "Tell me about your week, Marco," Victoria said, then added, "I haven't heard from you since last week."

Marco thought the line of inquiry was somewhat unusual. He wasn't planning on talking about him or his week. Plus, she had no idea his day job was social work.

Most people thought he worked at his foundation on a full-time basis. Marco thought that was best for his credibility. They wouldn't understand that he didn't want to take a salary from the foundation. That would leave less money to use for doing good.

"Most of my week involves helping others. I meet with community groups and seek individuals who need help," Marco said without getting into too many details. He didn't want to get caught in a lie.

As they walked, Marco noticed something. He saw it at the coffee shop last week, but it was much more frequent now. Everywhere they walked, people watched Victoria. Men turned their heads and stared at her as she walked down the street. But Marco noted it was not just the men. Women did it, too. Of course, Marco knew Victoria was an attractive woman. She was tall. At six feet, Marco was taller than many, but with her heels on, Victoria was actually taller than Marco.

What Marco didn't see was the black van parked on the street whose occupants had taken notice of Victoria, too.

With no prompting, Victoria started opening up to Marco. "I am so envious of you, Marco. You are doing exactly what you want. You have the freedom to pursue your own dreams. I'm stuck in a job where I seem to have zero motivation, working for my father's import company. I used to love going to work with him when I was younger. He would tell me, 'Someday, Victoria, you will run this company.' Now that he's gone, I don't want to even be there. It's too painful for me."

Marco was surprised by her candor. He hardly knew her, but her comments struck a chord with him and he thought back to working at the family bakery as a child. He, like Victoria, loved working with his dad. That all changed when his dad died as well. What a strange coincidence. He was too uncomfortable to share his own experience. This was a working relationship, and he didn't want to cross the line. Victoria obviously didn't feel the same about crossing that line and continued, "He died in a plane crash when I was twenty-four. The corporate jet was taking off from Denver in a snowstorm."

Marco's heart sank as he heard the pain in her voice. "I'm sorry you went through that. I know how difficult it is to lose someone so important in your life. It stays with you for a very long time." Victoria nodded in agreement and they walked along in silence, each deep in their own thoughts.

After walking for several more blocks, they stopped in front of a small, nondescript storefront. "We're here," he said, almost with a laugh. He envisioned the many high-end stores she frequented and what she was probably thinking now, standing in front of a secondhand clothing store. Before he could say anything, she flung open the door and stepped into the store. Her reaction was not at all what Marco expected. She quickly moved between racks of dresses, sweaters, and slacks, commenting on how cute this top was or how comfortable that sweater would have been.

"So what are we shopping for?" Victoria inquired with that same big smile on her face. Marco never noticed how perfectly straight and white her teeth were. And those eyes: bright blue eyes that stared right through you.

"This is a serious shopping trip, Victoria," Marco said, and Victoria pantomimed herself as she wiped the smile off her face.

"Okay, I'm being serious now," she said, then broke out into a giggle.

"We're shopping for you," Marco explained. "Tonight, we will be going into some pretty rough neighborhoods and I'm afraid your clothes won't work. They will make you a potential target. I have to make sure you make it home safely."

"Such a serious man, Marco," she said, fighting away a smile on her face. "But now that I know the occasion, let me see what I can find. It sounds like I should dress in a kind of street-chic style. Homeless crossed with Times

Square knockoff. I think I can pull it off."

With that, Victoria began examining the various items on racks and shelves, trying to find just the right outfit. At one point she fluttered back to Marco to give him her handbag to hold before heading off again. *What could she possibly have in here that's so heavy?* he wondered.

After twenty minutes, Victoria returned to Marco with an armful of clothing. He could tell she was having a good time and Marco thought, *Boy, it doesn't take much to keep her entertained.* She took him by the hand and led him to the dressing rooms, encouraging him to have a seat before disappearing behind a curtain.

After a few minutes of rustling, he heard a voice behind the curtain say, "Next up, we have Victoria in a cute little number designed by Chez Van Hough." The curtain flung open and Victoria walked out in a pair of jeans—complete with holes in the knees—a pink top with a matching sweater, and a pair of loafers. She strutted over to Marco and around his chair, waving her arms in the air before striking a pose in front of him. "What do you think?"

Without thinking, Marco blurted out "beautiful" and instantly regretted his choice of words. "I mean the outfit. It's a brilliant choice," he stammered. Victoria giggled again and walked around to the back of his chair. She put her hands on his shoulders, leaned down, and whispered, "Oh, I know what you meant," before strutting off behind the curtain again.

Five minutes later, she emerged wearing a tank top, a flannel shirt, and a pair of skinny jeans. She walked over to Marco and struck a different pose. This time Marco was ready and said in his most professional voice, "That works, too."

"I'll take both outfits," Victoria said, then continued, "You never know, Marco, I may want to come out with you more often." She took him by the hand and led him to the registers to pay for her new finds. Marco didn't want to admit it, but he was having a good time. He was still stuck on telling her she was beautiful. Truth be known, he wasn't wrong, and he knew it.

They exited the store and stopped on the sidewalk. Victoria had decided to wear the first outfit she tried on and stashed her other belongings, along with the second outfit, into two shopping bags that she handed to Marco. "Where to now?" Victoria asked.

"I have a big surprise for you," he responded. With that, they started their walk.

***

After having turned down an alley, Marco and Victoria stopped in front of a nondescript door. This, along with other doors, led into the businesses that fronted on the main street. It was a busy part of the neighborhood, near to where Victoria first parked her car. It surprised Marco how much he enjoyed his time with Victoria at the secondhand clothing shop, and although the conversation on the walk here was ordinary, he had to admit that he enjoyed that, too. It was nice having someone to talk to. He was connecting with Victoria, and that connection would pay off in the end. *Literally speaking*, he thought, and a smile crossed his face.

Marco knocked on the door. After a few minutes, he heard a commotion. Locks got unlocked and the door partially opened. Behind it stood a well-dressed man of about fifty. He was balding on top with long hair pulled into a ponytail. Standing at only five feet four, he was considerably shorter than Marco and looked up to him as the door swung open. The man saw Marco and exclaimed, "Marco! Where the hell have you been? I haven't seen you for a few weeks. How are you?"

"I'm good, Frankie. Thanks for letting us come over."

"Hell, Marco, you're always welcome here," Frankie responded, stepping forward to shake Marco's hand so vigorously that it rattled his jaw. "Where are my manners? You didn't tell me you were bringing someone tonight, especially someone so lovely," he continued, sidestepping Marco to stand directly in front of Victoria. "And who are we?"

"We are Victoria," she said with her electric smile on display. "Thank you for hosting us, although I don't know what for."

"Marco? In six years of knowing you, I have never seen you with a woman. Did you kidnap her?" He turned to Victoria and half whispered, "Did he drug you? The secret word can be 'pecans.' Say it and I'll have the cops here in two shakes of a cat's tail."

"Okay, okay, enough fun for now," Marco pined as he suggested they come in from the alley. Frankie waved them in and as they stepped in, he closed the door behind them and locked it. They walked into a well-lit storage area with supplies stacked neatly on shelves. Large bags of flour and sugar filled the shelves along with dozens of other cooking supplies. They walked down a corridor and around a corner into a room with several stainless-steel preparation tables in the middle. Along one end, there was a series of ovens and on another side was a dishwashing station that was not in operation. In fact, there weren't any other people there. They stopped in front of one of the prep tables. Frankie turned toward Marco and Victoria and extended his hand to Victoria, but she shook her head and refused to take it. Instead, she extended her arms, took a step forward, and wrapped them around Frankie, giving him a big hug.

"I warned Marco that I'm a touchy-feely person. It's so good to meet you," she said, releasing him and finishing with, "even though I have no idea who you are."

"I'm so sorry!" Frankie said as Marco stared at Frankie, unsure of how he felt about Victoria's hug and feeling confused about why he even cared. "Marco saved my life and I can never repay him."

Having recovered from the hug, Marco replied, "No, Frankie. I just gave you the opportunity. You were the one who took it."

"Is someone going to tell me a story, please?" Victoria pleaded.

Frankie continued, "I was living on the streets as a drug addict. I was homeless, penniless, and hopeless. I had considered ending my life many times but could never bring myself to do it. Victoria, I can't even tell you how bad it was. I stole money from family, friends, everyone. I went into my family home and took all their electronics while they were away on vacation. I sold them on the streets to pay for my drug habit. My family had me arrested, and I served time in state prison. I actually spent a fair amount of time there. After I lost access to my family, I started burglarizing other residences. Then I held up a liquor store, where the owner of the store shot me." Frankie gently tapped his upper right chest, showing her where the bullet went in. "I was lying on the cold floor, bleeding from my chest, just wishing for my life to end. I had hit rock bottom. While in prison, I met this guy," he said while rubbing Marco's shoulder. "He saved my life. We talked all the time. He would ask me what are my dreams? What did I love to do? The answer was simple. I love to cook. The only good memories I have as a child were cooking with my granny. She taught me everything she knew," he said, pausing to think about his granny, then kissing the crucifix hanging around his neck and pointing to the sky. "She was my world, and I let her down. She passed while I was locked up. I still get so aggravated at myself when I think about it."

Marco could see his story riveted Victoria. "I'm so sorry, Frankie," she said with her eyes misting over.

Frankie continued, "But Marco was a rock for me. He believed in me when no one else would. While I was in, he got me videos, books, and online cooking classes. After I got out, he put me up in a group home, supported me and got me more training. He paid for everything. It turned my life around." Victoria looked over at Marco with a warm smile. He thought to himself, *You wanted me exposed, well here I am.* He was proud of the story that Frankie was telling, but for once he wasn't thinking about how much money it may earn him. He was glad that Frankie shared it with Victoria.

"Is this restaurant yours?" Victoria inquired.

"It sure is. Except for the part that the bank owns, of course. But I'm making money, paying the bank back and paying the people back who I hurt. Including my family." Frankie hesitated, then softly said, "And they forgave me."

Victoria leaned in and gave Frankie another hug. "Thanks so much for telling me your story, Frankie. It's so inspiring."

"This guy gets anything he wants. I would walk across broken glass barefoot for him," Frankie said as he motioned toward Marco.

"Frankie, thanks so much for telling Victoria your story."

"No problem. I know you two have work to do, so I'll leave you alone. Let me know if you need anything," Frankie said as he walked toward the front of the restaurant.

When he was no longer in sight, Victoria looked at Marco and mouthed, *That's amazing*. Marco beamed with pride.

"We have lots of things to do and not a lot of time. We're going to be baking. It's something that I really enjoy doing," he said. "But don't ask why. That will come later."

"Why?" Victoria responded. "Not why are we doing it, but why can't I ask?" She ended with a big childlike grin. Marco just shook his head as he began gathering the supplies they needed.

"We're going to bake cookies," he said and over the next twenty minutes, explained the process and described the ingredients needed to make them. They worked together to gather what they needed, with Marco directing her to different shelves.

On the way back from one of her trips, Marco saw that Victoria appeared to want to say something but was holding back. He was not sure he wanted to encourage her to say what was on her mind since she sometimes said things with high shock value that were highly personal. He remembered that look from their coffee meeting when she asked him about growing up. Their eyes met, and she seemed to read in them a green light. Before Marco could divert his gaze, she stopped across the table from him and asked, "Marco, have you ever had a relationship with anyone? I mean a genuine relationship. As an adult."

Marco knew something personal was coming, but even so, this question caught him completely by surprise. His natural reflex was to say, "Why do you ask?" He wondered if he was being too defensive with his response.

"I'm exceptionally good at reading people. I was just wondering. And Frankie said…"

She trailed off, but Marco finished her sentence, "That I have never brought anyone around in six years." Victoria nodded her head in agreement.

"Maybe a date or two here and there, but nothing serious. I am too busy trying to build my foundation."

"Hmmm," Victoria said and left the pause in the conversation hanging as if expecting some confession from Marco. He answered the question honestly, he thought. There wasn't anything else to tell. She came around the same side of the table as Marco and looked him in the eyes. "You know, Marco, you need to make time for yourself. To build a life outside of your work. To have meaningful, loving relationships in your life. Your foundation won't be around forever," Victoria spoke in such a soft and heartfelt way that it caught him by surprise. He didn't respond and after a minute, she turned around and headed back to the shelf for another ingredient.

As he put the ingredients into a gigantic bowl, he noticed how much he and Victoria were in each other's personal space. Often, it was necessary, but sometimes he noticed that Victoria enjoyed crowding him a little. She rubbed against him, then gave him a sheepish grin, saying, "Oh, sorry," when she brushed against him in an obvious way. Marco was not used to cooking as a duo. For him, it was a solitary activity and always had been since his dad passed away. It was his time to think and reflect. But sharing the kitchen with Victoria had a comfortable feel to it, and he was enjoying it.

He was not sure why he asked, but after taking a deep breath, Marco returned the favor to Victoria. "What about you? Have you had many serious relationships?" He almost regretted asking it as soon as the words left his mouth.

"A few. They were all 'approved' for me by my mother," she said, using her fingers to form air quotes around the word "approved." "Because of my upbringing, she feels the need to involve herself in every aspect of my life, including that one." She continued making trips to the shelves as she spoke. "But I'm old enough to make my own decisions. I know what I want in life. I want to love someone for who they are, not what they have, and poor Mrs. Van Hough is done directing my life."

Hearing her mom's name was like a small electric shock to his brain. He had gotten lost in the night and forgotten about his purpose. He felt like he had let himself down a little and vowed to stay with his plan. These personal conversations got him sidetracked. Not anymore, he thought.

Marco retrieved containers of yellow, purple, red, and pink frosting that he opened and placed on the table where they were working. "We'll use these to frost the cookies," he said as he switched on the mixer. He watched as the machine roared to life, combining the efforts of their hard work so far. As the mixing progressed, Marco noticed that Victoria was leaning with the full weight of her body against his back. She was looking over his shoulder, mesmerized by the rhythmic motion of the mixing blades. Her left hand rested on his left shoulder, and he felt her breath on his neck. He didn't move, content to stand there without words, feeling her body next to his.

When the dough was the perfect consistency, Marco stopped the mixer and instructed Victoria on how to remove it. He divided it in half and after flouring the table in front of them, he placed each ball of dough on the table. "We have to use the rolling pin to roll out the dough to a nice, even thickness." He took one of the rolling pins they had gathered earlier and began to demonstrate. "Look. It's easy," he said as he skillfully rolled back and forth, occasionally lifting the sheet of dough and rotating it ninety degrees before rolling again. He looked over at Victoria and saw she hadn't begun rolling her dough. "Something wrong?" he asked.

"No, it just isn't as easy as you make it look," she replied.

"Watch me," he said as he showed her again. Victoria took her rolling pin and tried rolling out the dough just like Marco. With each roll, the dough wrapped around her rolling pin. She pulled it off the rolling pin and tried again. Marco watched her with his peripheral vision with amusement. He assumed that Victoria hadn't had problems with anything she had tried in the past. And if she had, there was probably some domestic help nearby to assist. He smiled at the thought.

"What's so funny?" Victoria asked, but he couldn't tell her of the amusing scene that played out in his mind. "You think this is funny?" she said as the corners of her lips rose in a stifled smile.

"I have a better way for you to show me," Victoria said, as she lifted his right arm and slipped in front of him, between Marco and the preparation table. Then she lowered his arm and placed his hand on the table, surrounding her with him. While facing the table, she took his hands and placed them on the ends of the rolling pin with hers on top of his. "Now show me."

Her rather bold move surprised him. There she was, in front of him with her hands on his. Marco's body felt stiff and unnatural as they rolled the dough together. At first, the dough wrapped around the rolling pin, just as it did with Victoria. "Hey!" she said. "Do it right."

Marco focused on the rolling motion. Back and forth,

rolling together. Her soft hands were on top of his, now with their fingers intertwined. He noticed his body relaxing and the awkwardness fading away. He shuffled forward so that the front of his body was completely touching Victoria's back. She released her hands and with great skill, took her long blond hair, wrapping it around and securing it in a messy bun on top of her head. "That's better," she said, rubbing her body gently against his, trying to settle back between his arms. She put her hands back on his and interlaced their fingers again, and the rolling began again. Marco failed to notice that the dough rolling was going nowhere. He lowered his head, resting his chin gently on her shoulder, and leaned his head against hers. For the first time, he noticed her scent, taking it in and exhaling deeply. This caused Victoria to moan slightly and begin swaying back and forth, rubbing softly against Marco. Back and forth, they swayed to some imaginary tune playing in their heads.

Slowly, Victoria released her hands and pushed back against Marco, making space between them. She turned around, so they were staring into each other's eyes. Reflexively, Marco stopped rolling and put his hands on her hips, pulling her closer to him. They were so close now. Her lips were wet, and he wanted them to meet his. Marco was unskilled in this area and wasn't sure what to do next. He closed his eyes, waiting for them to meet. He felt something on his lips, but it didn't feel like the sweet kiss he was expecting.

He opened his eyes to see Victoria smiling at him. He touched his lips and looked at his hand. On his fingers, he saw purple frosting. Looking down, he saw Victoria's hand, covered in purple frosting, and she gave him an enormous smile. Marco was as confused as he had ever been. What was going on? he thought. But before he could gather his thoughts, Victoria took her hand and smeared more purple frosting on the side of his face. Taking advantage of his shock, she ducked under his arm and scurried to the other side of the table. She took a small ball of dough, wadded it up and launched it at Marco, hitting him in the chest.

Marco snapped out of the hypnotic trance she put him in and reverted back to his street senses. He knew what was going on. One time, when he was six, he and his brothers engaged in such a battle. This was a food fight. More specifically, a frosting fight. He scanned the table, assessing the availability of ammunition. Four containers. He looked up and his eyes met Victoria's. She was on to him. Marco extended his long arms out across the table. Victoria sensed what he was doing and extended her arms as well. In one swoop, Marco swept three of the four frosting containers into his arms, leaving only the pink one for Victoria. She quickly retrieved it to her side, digging in for the first salvo. In one motion, she dipped her hands into the container and flung frosting toward Marco. It flew true, leaving a trail of pink across the table until it hit its mark: a big pink splotch on Marco's chest. He looked down. "Damn," he whispered. "You got me."

Marco returned fire from the red frosting container and hit Victoria in the forehead. "Hey!" she exclaimed, picking up her container and advancing on him. He selected the red and purple containers and carried them as he retreated around the table. Victoria advanced as she fired multiple handfuls of frosting, hitting him in the shoulder and stomach. She was adept at dodging and only took one additional hit to her arm. The battle continued as Victoria ran out of frosting and resorted to lobbing dough balls at Marco.

Just as she was running out of things to throw, they heard a noise at the entrance to the kitchen. They turned to see Frankie shaking his head. He smiled and said, "It's probably a good thing you never brought anyone else here!" He laughed as he walked away.

The two of them broke out into laughter, having agreed to a cease-fire. "We better clean this place up," Marco said.

"What about the cookies?" Victoria asked.

"No time, but no worries. We can stop and buy some,"

he said, shooting her a smile.

Together they worked in relative silence to clean up the mess. Each left to their own thoughts. Marco wasn't sure what to think, but he was past his doubt of what Allison had said about Victoria's intentions. The only problem was Marco didn't know what his intensions were. Until a little while ago, he wasn't sure that Victoria was even interested. Besides, he didn't have the time to dedicate to a relationship, did he? He had to stay focused on the foundation.

Frankie poked his head in and saw the progress being made. "Just leave those dishes in the sink over there," he said, pointing to the washing station, and walked away.

They wrapped up the cleaning and proceeded to clean themselves. Victoria took her handbag and went into the bathroom while Marco washed up in the cooking sink. He finished before her and sat to wait. When she rounded the corner back to the kitchen, Marco was again struck by her beauty. Then he saw the frosting stains still on her sweater and laughed.

She walked over to him and said, "I'm not sure what you're laughing about, frosty," pointing to the pink stains on his shirt. They laughed, and she slipped into his arms and gave him a warm hug. She released her grip and pulled away, and he longed for a kiss. *Strange*, he thought.

They thanked Frankie and quickly found themselves, without cookies, standing in the alley. "Where to now?" she asked.

"You'll see," Marco responded and directed them down the alley to the street, turning left. They headed toward the unsafe part of town, and Marco hoped this portion of the evening was life changing for her. He was oblivious to the black van parked near the corner. The headlights switched on as they walked by.

CHAPTER NINE
Victoria

After walking through the alley, they turned left down the street where Marco directed them. It was dark out and Victoria looked at her watch. Seven thirty. She was on cloud nine. She couldn't believe how much she was enjoying herself. First the shopping trip, then baking and now, who-knew-what. These clothes weren't the kind she normally wore, but after looking in the fitting room mirror, she thought she still looked fabulous. She was not sure why this was necessary, but she was a go-with-the-flow kind of gal. According to Marco, they would be going into some rough neighborhoods. *How tough could it be?* she wondered. She had friends growing up who didn't live in gated communities like her, and she didn't have problems there.

Then the baking. That was amazing. Victoria thought about it as they walked. She was not sure what came over her to make her put frosting on Marco's face. It just seemed right. Not that she didn't want to enjoy their first kiss. She really wanted to, but she was someone who enjoyed having fun and couldn't resist putting frosting on his face. It was an enormous risk for her. Some men she dated in the past couldn't handle her silly spontaneity, but luckily Marco took it in stride. That only reinforced in her mind that he was a catch. But Victoria had a nagging question that she would have to answer if this relationship was going to progress. *Why hadn't he dated before?* she wondered. His foundation? Was it just that simple, or was there something more? Despite the many dating fails she had experienced, Victoria knew that each one helped her sort out the things she wanted in a partner, and the things she didn't want. More times than not, they were the latter, but still important. Of course, there was one man in her life before, Nate, who Victoria still remembered with fondness, but that was several years ago. Their lives had just moved in different directions, and she had moved on from him. As painful as that had been.

Victoria brushed those memories aside and refocused on Marco. She had other questions as well, and this seemed like the perfect time to ask them. She knew this might have been uncomfortable for Marco and remembered when they had coffee together. The questions she asked about growing up seemed to make him squirm, so she eased him into it.

"I really enjoyed myself, Marco. Thank you. Too bad we weren't able to bake anything," she said with a half smile. "You told me you worked for the family bakery when you were growing up, right?"

She noticed that Marco had a slightly discernable grimace on his face as she asked the question. This was obviously a difficult situation for him. "Yes. My parents came here from Italy and started a bakery before I was born. My earliest memories are of working there with my father. He taught me everything I know."

"You really light up when you talk about your dad. He must have been a wonderful man," Victoria said, trying to get him to open up further. So far, everything had been surface-type information. She wanted to go deeper with him.

"Well, he was far from perfect, but I really loved him," Marco continued.

Victoria said, "My father was the same. He meant the

world to me, but he wasn't perfect, either. He strayed on my mom and she will never forgive him, but my relationship with him was different." Victoria hoped that by opening up to him, she could connect with Marco. His face seemed to soften up a little.

"My father had his problems," Marco said, then allowed a significant pause before taking a deep breath and continuing. "I have never talked about this to anyone." Victoria reached down and took his hand in hers, and Marco continued, "A few years after coming here, he got mixed up with the wrong people. He already was a heavy drinker, but he started doing drugs. At first, he was able to continue running the bakery while partying all night. But eventually, he stopped doing anything except the drugs and alcohol. He was gone for days at a time, so all the responsibility fell on my mom. She had my brothers who were fairly young at the time, so she took them to the bakery with her during the day."

"I'm so sorry, Marco," Victoria said and squeezed his hand.

They had walked about eight blocks and made several turns as directed by Marco. The crowd on the street had thinned considerably. They walked through a transition neighborhood. Developers were discovering it and investing money here, but it was a far cry from where they came.

"This went on for many years. Dad had several overdoses, and a few times, it involved the police. This was all before I was born. He had one particularly bad overdose where he died, but they brought him back. After that, my dad swore off drugs and alcohol. He recommitted himself to my mother, my brothers, my sister, and the bakery. They had another child as a sign of their recommitment to each other."

"And that child was you?" Victoria asked.

"That's right. The first twelve years of my life were the best. I baked with my father in the mornings and on weekends. He taught me everything. How to bake, run a business, how to love and about forgiveness."

"Marco, I have a feeling this story doesn't have a happy ending," Victoria said with a frown.

"I wish it did. Around the time of my thirteenth birthday, Dad started acting strange. He would lose his temper easily, and his personality changed. He was angry all the time. Mom knew the signs immediately and confronted him. He fell back into his old habits." Marco took another long pause, seeming to gather his thoughts before continuing, "I remember the first time he overdosed. I sat at his bedside and cried. The hospital treated him like an addict. A common junkie. 'He's just going to do it again,' they would say. 'We're wasting our time and resources on him.' I could hear them talking in the hallway. There were no programs available to help him, so I watched him spiral down to the bottom. It was heartbreaking for a thirteen-year-old boy." Marco went quiet. Victoria wondered if he was just lost in his thoughts. She decided to not push him anymore. She was getting a picture of him and a better understanding.

They had walked about fifteen blocks, but Victoria hadn't noticed how the neighborhood had changed again. The cute businesses that morphed into the transition neighborhood had changed again. Now they walked down streets lined with pawnshops and liquor stores. Bars covered the windows, with roll-down gates over the doors. The streets had a foul smell. The sidewalks under the bridges were dotted with homeless encampments. Those who were lucky had tents with ropes that stretched out to telephone poles or fences offering support. Marco directed Victoria around these, causing her to take stock of her surroundings. It shocked her to see how the neighborhood had changed and how its residents were living. Those without tents took shelter in structures made of cardboard, shipping pallets, shopping carts, or anything they could find on the streets. The unluckiest, the lowest of the low in this social circle, slept on the ground covered in filthy clothes to keep warm. There were squabbles that broke out as they walked by, with people yelling obscenities at each other. One man urinated next to a tent, and another man had a tourniquet on his arm, preparing to inject something. These were shocking sights to Victoria. Ones she had never seen in her life. She was not sure she enjoyed being so close to the action, but Marco held her close and she felt safe with him.

As they walked, Victoria saw that a few of the men had taken notice of them and seemed to follow behind. She looked around, feeling extremely nervous. "It's okay. I'm with you. Stay close to me," Marco said in a reassuring voice, and Victoria felt a little better. At the next street corner, there was a barrel fire burning with several men standing around it. As they approached the barrel, two of the men turned and looked at Marco and Victoria. They stepped into their path.

"Pretty girl," one man said, looking her up and down in a way that made Victoria's skin crawl. They all came to a stop. The man reached out his hand to touch Victoria's hair, but Marco shoved it away. Without taking his eyes off the men, Marco reached his hand behind him and located Victoria. He nudged her behind him and stood tall in front of them. She reasoned that he used his over six-foot frame to intimidate them. It seemed to work as the men backed down and moved out of the way for them to pass. Victoria was thankful to have Marco with her.

"We're almost there," he said to her as they rounded the next corner. They stopped in front of a dilapidated old building that used to be a storefront. Green paint was peeling on all the surfaces, and boards covered some windows. The remaining windows and doors had bars on them. They walked up to the door, opened it, and were met immediately by a large man. He saw Marco and broke out into a smile. He stepped forward and embraced him.

"Marco!" he exclaimed. "Nice to see you, man. It's been a while."

"The last few times I was here, you weren't," Marco replied, releasing his grip on the man and stepping back.

"Remember that lead you gave me about the security officer's position? Well, I got the job," the man continued beaming with pride. "Now I only volunteer here a few times a month."

Marco told him, "That's amazing. I'm so happy for you."

"Thanks. But you better come in, it's getting a little rough out there tonight," he said, stepping aside and clearing a path for them to enter.

As she entered, Victoria walked into a world she had never experienced before. She looked around a large room containing dozens of people, mostly women and children. To the left, there was a series of banquet tables and chairs all lined up. A half-dozen children were running around and between the tables, playing a game of tag. They yelled and screamed, occasionally getting scolded by their respective parent. Behind them, Victoria saw what looked like a commercial kitchen with two large stoves, cabinets, and two refrigerators. Several adults were in the kitchen washing and drying dishes. To the right was a hallway leading to another part of the building, and in front of that, tattered couches and chairs organized in a circle. It looked like a meeting was taking place there. There was an open chair in the circle near Victoria, and the leader of the group looked up at her and extended his hand.

"I'm Tom. Have a seat and join us," he said, pointing to the open chair.

Victoria looked over at Marco, who said, "Victoria, this is Tom. He works with the residents on life skills. I told him you were coming with me tonight. Why don't you join the group? It will give you a chance to experience what they do." He released her hand and walked over to the open chair. Victoria went over and sat down. She watched Marco walk over to the kitchen and greet some volunteers working there. Tom's voice caused her to turn her attention back to the group.

"Thanks for joining the group, Victoria. Marco has told us a lot about you. Your skills would be especially helpful here," Tom said. "I work in human resources for a large employer in the area. Marco recruited me to come help. This shelter works with a lot of women who are able to leave their abusive relationships. Other counselors work with them on mental health issues, but I focus on life skills. Many of these women have to manage a household, get a job, and work through various government programs to name a few. It can be extremely intimidating for some. Tonight, we are talking about getting a job. Many of the women have minimal skills so we work with them and various employment agencies to help them learn interview skills, create a résumé, and get a job."

Victoria felt a little overwhelmed by all this information. "I'm not sure what to say, Tom. I grew up in a world where these skills were provided, almost expected."

"I know exactly where you're coming from, Victoria. I was in the same place four years ago when I first walked in that door. It's unfortunate, but we are trying to make a difference for as many of these women as we can. Let's get going, okay?"

He addressed a woman in the first chair. Victoria guessed she was only in her twenties but appeared much older. Life had not been kind to her, Victoria suspected. "Hi, Cathy, how's your résumé coming along?" Cathy handed it to Tom. He looked it over and handed it to Victoria. She scanned it from top to bottom and noted there was nothing under the heading *Work Experience.*

"Hi, Cathy, I'm Victoria. Tell me about your work experience. Have you ever had a job before?"

Cathy seemed embarrassed, and Victoria felt like she might have been too harsh in how she asked the question. She was used to working with executive-level people, so this was new for her. Victoria followed up with, "I'm sorry if that was harsh. I'm not judging you, Cathy. I'm just trying to find things to put on your résumé."

"It's okay. I understand, It's just hard." Cathy started to cry. Victoria reached her hand out and took Cathy's. Her hands felt so rough, and Victoria thought about how different their lives were. Before today, Victoria's biggest concern was getting her new designer handbag. Now she wondered what life was really about.

"How about when you were younger?" Victoria continued.

"Well, I worked at a fast-food restaurant while in high school. Then I worked in an office before getting pregnant for the first time," she explained.

"Excellent. We can use that. Let's add those right here," Victoria said as she worked through the résumé changes with Cathy. Next, she worked with a woman on interview skills while Tom worked with two others.

After wrapping up, Victoria took a deep breath and looked across the room to find Marco. She was surprised to see him sitting on a chair across the room to her left. Around him were four laughing children. One child was pretending to cut his hair, one was pretending to put makeup on him, and the other two were jumping up and down and laughing. It warmed Victoria's heart to see this side of Marco. He had such a kind soul. She had loved seeing everything he did for others. She thought back to her previous relationships. These men came from money. The kind of men her mother wanted for her. But they were so controlling. They weren't interested in making her a partner in their relationship. She was a trophy to be displayed on their arms at the various social events. But Victoria wanted more from her life. She wanted a partner and after seeing Marco in action, she was sure he could fit the bill. She laughed out loud. "I told him I wanted to see him in action, and here he is," she said. Victoria continued watching Marco as he laughed along with the children. He turned his head toward Victoria. Their eyes met, and he gave her a warm smile that made her melt.

Victoria's concentration was broken by a loud noise

coming from the back room. She turned her head to look, but only heard loud voices yelling, swearing, and glass breaking. The laughing stopped, and the children ran to the protection of their mothers' arms. Marco closed the distance between him and Victoria just as the commotion spilled out from the back room. A disheveled-looking man stumbled out from down the hall, followed closely behind by two large men wearing *STAFF* T-shirts.

"You know the rules, Harry. No drugs in the shelter. You broke the rules and now you have to leave," the men calmly told him. Harry stopped in the middle of the room and turned toward the men.

"I'm not leaving!" Harry said as he took a slow, winding swing of his fist at the staff members. The men both took a step back and easily dodged the haymaker from the impaired man. He lost his balance and fell on the tables, taking several of them down in a crash. Cups and pitchers of water went flying across the room, and several small children cried out. The two large men helped Harry back to his feet and aggressively moved him to the door. The man at the door opened it up, and they pushed Harry out onto the sidewalk. The two staff members stepped out, and the door closed behind them.

The commotion reduced the bustling shelter to silence except for the sound of mothers comforting their crying babies. Victoria noticed that in the melee, Marco had once again put himself in between her and the danger. She wrapped her arms around him as he faced the room. He turned around and pulled her toward him, holding her tight. She felt so safe in his arms and took a few moments to soak it in. "Let's help clean up and we can go," he whispered to her, and she nodded in agreement.

Together, they worked to upright the tables, replace the plastic tablecloths, and pick up the cups and pitchers and put them in the sink. They waved goodbye and moved to the door to leave. Marco opened the door and looked out to assess the situation. "No need to walk out into a problem, right?" he said to Victoria before exiting the shelter. They turned right and retraced their steps back to Victoria's car. As they passed the homeless encampment where Marco had been so brave, she noticed how much quieter it was now.

"Where did they all go?" she asked Marco. He pointed to the tents, sleeping bags, cardboard boxes, and bundles of rags. Only a few men mingled around on the sidewalks, but that was enough to make Victoria concerned as she reached for Marco's hand and squeezed it tight.

As they walked, it seemed to Victoria that Marco was deep in his thoughts. He seemed content to let them simply absorb the night's events. The neighborhoods transitioned back as they walked. From bars on the windows all the way back to thriving businesses full of energy. Victoria became lost in her own thoughts. Tonight had been a wonderful night. She enjoyed getting to know Marco better, and although he seemed to be somewhat reserved with the information he shared, she had a good feeling about his character. He seemed like a good man, and she wanted to get to know him better. She had to admit that things got a little sticky, but that was Marco's world and she was willing to be there with him, if it gave her a chance to get to know him better. She was already thinking about the possibility of a next date as they approached her car parked on the curb where they had left it so many hours ago.

Victoria stepped off the curb and leaned against her car, facing Marco. With only a slight tug for incentive, Marco moved in front of her and she buried herself in his chest. Marco wrapped his arms around her and held her tight. He took his fingers and ran them through her hair, and she exhaled deeply at his touch. *This is exactly where I want to be,* Victoria thought while enjoying the feel of him stroking her hair.

"It's getting late," Marco said.

Victoria took her face away from his chest and looked up into his eyes. "When will I see you again?" she asked, choosing her words carefully to convey the message it was a matter of when, not if. Because that was what she wanted. She was sure he did, too. As they stared into each other's eyes, Victoria longed for their first kiss. Now was the time. No frosting fights, no interruptions, just the kiss she had been waiting patiently for. *Why isn't he moving?* she wondered. She wanted to kiss him, but he was not moving. Finally, after what felt like an eternity, she tired of waiting. She took her arms from around his waist and draped them around his neck, pulling him forward. Their lips met and Victoria moaned softly. It was exactly what she had been waiting for, and she had to guard against her legs getting weak. Soft, moist lips on hers and she ran her fingers through his hair. She felt Marco pull her closer. She was letting herself go as she got lost in the moment when suddenly he stopped. Marco pulled his head back from her.

"Victoria, it's getting late," he said.

Victoria's world stopped turning as disappointment washed over her. She wasn't sure what she expected as an outcome, but this wasn't it. She smiled at Marco, stood on her tiptoes, and gave one last, brief kiss.

"Call me, but don't make me wait too long," she whispered as she broke free from his grasp, turning around and opening her car door.

"Have a safe drive home, Victoria," Marco said as he closed her door behind her.

Victoria pulled down her visor mirror and took a long look in it, then fluffed her blond mane. She closed it and looked out the window as she started her car. Marco had moved back to the sidewalk, and she waved goodbye to him as she pulled away.

Neither of them noted that a black van parked down the street switched on their lights and pulled out a few cars behind Victoria. She turned right. So did the van.

CHAPTER TEN
Victoria

Victoria was still basking in the glow of the previous night as she sat in a deck chair by the swimming pool situated on their expansive family compound. It was fall and the pool service had long since closed it for the season, but she still liked to take advantage of days like these by sitting on the deck. She looked around and saw the landscapers had recently done their work on the many shrubs, grasses, and plants dotting the grounds. The sun was shining, and she enjoyed feeling the warmth on her face. It surprised her at how quickly she fell for Marco, but when it was right, it was right. Victoria had been waiting so long for someone like this in her life. All the failed relationships and horrible men she endured. Not that they abused her. They weren't alcoholics or drug addicts, but they weren't interested in her. They didn't want to build a life together with common goals and dreams. They were about their own dreams, and Victoria was just along for the ride. She was the window dressing of sorts for their lives. She was their hood ornament. But Victoria knew she wanted more out of life than that. Yes, she would have lived in comfort for the rest of her life. Luxury that she was accustomed to having, but as she got older, she realized that money wasn't everything.

She picked up her cell phone. The screen brightened, and the main screen appeared. She swiped to her text messages, looked, and sighed. Nothing yet. "Patience," she said out loud. She was sure Marco was a busy man and might take some time to respond.

She closed her eyes and thought back to their first kiss. She replayed their lips coming together and remembered the feel of them. They were so soft, warm, and moist. Like pillows. And he was such a good kisser. She couldn't wait to kiss him again. She was proud of herself for taking matters into her own hands to make that kiss happen, but wondered why she had to be the one to start. She recalled some other guys she dated and how she frequently referred to them as octopi. So many arms, she thought. But she knew that Marco was a bit naïve when it came to intimate relationships, having had so few in his life. Victoria didn't mind being the one to drive intimacy. She was exceedingly confident in her sexuality and was the perfect person to teach Marco. *We could grow together*, she thought.

She scooped up her phone and headed down the walking path back to the house. She opened the door to the solarium that covered a third of the back of the mansion and stepped inside.

"Good morning, Ms. Victoria," said a middle-aged man who walked past her and out the back door.

"Hi, John!" Victoria said to the staff member who coordinated all maintenance and repairs to the house and grounds. She continued into the breakfast room and took a seat, looking out the back windows where she had a beautiful view of the backyard and pool to the right and the gardens to the left. She loved this view but thought it was a bit of a waste of space. Only two people lived in nearly 20,000 square feet with a staff of six. She shook her head. But that was what Mom wanted. Ever since Dad passed away, she refused to downsize. But Victoria wasn't sure why, since, in the end, she hated him.

A voice from behind her caused Victoria to jump. She

turned around to see Helen, a member of the staff.

"Hi, Ms. Victoria, can I get you anything? Are you interested in having lunch?"

She looked at her watch. Noon. Her trainer would be here soon. "I'm good, thanks," she said as Helen nodded and made her way out of the room. She hated to exercise but loved how she looked. She frequently admired her figure in the mirror after her workout. *I wish there was an easier way*, she thought as she got up to go get ready.

On her way, she passed the double doors of the sitting room and saw her mother in her chair.

"Oh, Victoria dear, can I have a word with you?" her mother asked.

"Damn it," Victoria whispered under her breath. She was clearly not happy about being summoned to the principal's office. She wondered why her mother couldn't have half the house and Victoria the other half. There was plenty enough staff to go around, and they would all have been so much happier.

She backed up and peered into the room that served as her father's library. Over the years, he decorated it ornately with high-backed leather sitting chairs, mahogany tables, and two stories of mahogany shelves lined with books and more books. Ladders on rollers, made of beautiful wrought iron lined the room, reaching up to the top-most shelves. As a child, she would stand on the ladders as her dad rolled her back and forth. Victoria would laugh endlessly. As she got older, her dad taught her all about the rare books he collected and displayed in this room. She has read most of the classics: *A Bend in the River, Don Quixote,* and *The Scarlet Letter.* Many of them were first editions, and some of them remained in the collection. Except for Dad's favorites, which mom sold long ago, at a discount, of course. Just because.

"Come in, darling. I want to talk to you," she said, beckoning her into the room. She was sitting in her usual chair reading the newspaper and didn't even look up as she spoke. Victoria shuddered at those words. She knew her mother had an ulterior motive. She only had to wait for it to be revealed. She went in the room and sat in the chair opposite her mother.

"How are you doing, Mom? Don't we see each other enough at work? Why ruin a good thing by talking at home?" she said, with a heavy dose of sarcasm.

"I'm doing fine, dear. Thanks for asking," her mother responded with a frown. She put the newspaper down and lit a cigarette, finally looking across at Victoria. "Oh, Helen, would you bring us some tea, please?" she said to no one in particular. Suddenly, Helen appeared at the door.

"Right away, ma'am," Helen said before scurrying off. The staff did that all the time. Victoria often wondered if they always stayed within earshot to provide better service, or if they were eavesdropping to write a tell-all book after they retired. Either way, it made her uneasy.

Most often, Victoria didn't have patience and tried to get right to the point with her mother, but today, she was in the mood for games. Victoria decided she wouldn't take the bait. Instead, she was going to make her mother work for whatever information she wanted. They sat in silence while her mom smoked until Helen returned with a silver tray service and tea for two. She fixed each cup exactly how they liked it, then left the room. Victoria liked Helen. She had been with the family for as long as she could remember. She picked up the cup and took a sip, content with the silence in the room. *The games we play*, she thought.

"You were out late last night. What time did you get home?" she asked as an opening question that started them down the rabbit hole.

"I'm pretty sure you know exactly what time I got home," Victoria responded, knowing that as she entered the compound through the front drive gate, it triggered a security camera. There was a complete set of monitors in the master bedroom along with her panic room.

"Yes, of course I do. You know I don't sleep well, and

when I heard the gate buzzer, I had to go see who was at the gate. Out with your friends, I suppose?" she continued and stubbed out her cigarette. Victoria thought that was the most disgusting habit a person could ever have.

"A friend, yes," Victoria responded. "Why do you ask?" She realized that her defensive attitude had helped her mom enjoy this line of questioning more and vowed to not repeat that mistake.

"Well, I was wondering. Helen!" she called out. A minute later Helen showed up carrying a small pile of clothes neatly folded and put them on the table next to her mom. "Thanks, Helen," she said, and Helen disappeared back into the hallway. Victoria immediately recognized the clothes on the table as the ones Marco bought for her yesterday, but she was careful to not give away anything through facial tells. Her mom held up the sweater, and it unfolded in front of her, bringing back memories of all the fun she had last night. She fought away a smile. "Do these belong to you? I was looking at them and they aren't your brand. When did you start shopping at discount stores?" she said with a smirk. "I didn't peg you as a fan of the Gap," and a smile finally migrated across her face.

"Boy, Helen didn't waste any time washing them. Or giving them to you," she said.

"Now, dear, she's just doing her job, which she does exceptionally well, I might add."

"The washing or the ratting-out part?" Victoria replied, unable to hide her annoyance.

"Oh, honey," she said, letting her words drift off. "What kind of friend do you have who requires you to dress like this?" she said as she stretched her arm out over the pile of clothes. She waited for Victoria to confirm what she already knew, but Victoria didn't give her the satisfaction.

"Okay, well if I had to guess—"

Victoria interrupted her by saying, "But you don't have to guess now, do you?"

"Of course not, dear. When it comes to you, I make it

my job to know everything. You are my only daughter and my only child. Can I give you some advice?" When she asked permission to do something, she was going to do it anyway. =Victoria didn't respond, so she continued, "We have a class system. People of similar classes associate while people of lower classes associate with each other. These two shall not meet. Ever. Do you know what I'm saying?" Victoria knew exactly what she meant, but played along without acknowledging. "We are members of a certain class that we achieved through years of hard work, sacrifice, and dedication. Others want to join our exclusive group, but not by hard work. They seek opportunities to, how does your generation say it, 'hook up' with someone like us. They contribute nothing to the relationship and instead suck us dry."

Victoria felt her face flush. She was getting upset but needed to keep it under control. She refused to play into her mother's agenda. Any man who was ever acceptable to her mother was from an extraordinarily wealthy family. No exceptions. All the terrible memories of the dates of the past came back to the surface, but she pushed them back down. She refused to let her mom win.

"I warned you at the fundraiser, dear. I could see that look in your eyes. You always fall for the wrong guy. I don't fault you. You get that from your father. All his conquests were low class. Except me, of course, but it was downhill after that. I tolerated it, but I still don't know why," her mother said. This line of commentary pushed Victoria's buttons. Her mother knew that and did it intentionally. Victoria couldn't hold back.

"Don't you dare say anything about my father. He was a loving man, and you won't tarnish my feelings for him with your acidic comments. Just keep them to yourself." Victoria resisted saying what she wanted to say, out of respect for her mother, but her feelings were hurt. *Classy, Mom,* she thought to herself.

"Anyway, I don't want to argue with you," her mother

said. "All I'm saying is that he may be an exceedingly nice man, but he's in a different class. A lower class than people like us, and that will not work."

Victoria regained her composure and went back to her silent routine, making her mom work for it. "I'm sensing that my words are not getting through to you, honey. I have something else to share with you. As I said, I saw the way you looked at him at the fundraiser and figured it would come to this. So, I wanted to get to know him myself. I invited him to my office for a meeting with the promise of a donation to his foundation. He's quite a looker, I have to admit.

"After our meeting, I did a little checking," her mom continued as she pulled a file folder out from beside her chair. "I would never donate to someone without checking them out first, and with your obvious interest in him, I had an even more important reason. I want you to check this out," she said as she tried handing the folder to Victoria. "Then I want you to forget about him." Victoria refused to take the folder.

"Dear. Don't make this more difficult than it needs to be. I'll give you some highlights. His foundation is small potatoes. There is a financial statement in the folder." Victoria didn't bother asking her how she got a copy of his financials. She knew her mother had important contacts, deep pockets and a lot of motivation. She slid the folder across the small table in between their chairs, but Victoria still didn't take it. "He has no office space listed and one employee," she continued. "His total net worth is less than what we pay the gardener in a year."

Just in the nick of time, Helen came to the door. She peeked in and said, "I'm sorry to interrupt, ma'am, but Ms. Victoria's fitness trainer is waiting for her in the gym."

This was the opening she needed, and Victoria jumped up to leave. "Sorry, Mom, I have to go. Time is money!" She went around the table, kissed her mother on the cheek, and left the room. She could hear her mother in the background as she went, "You need to listen to me, Victoria!" But she was already halfway down the hall.

At the end of the hallway, she felt a vibration in her pocket and a feeling of warmth came over her. She knew who was texting and she couldn't wait to see what he said. She knew it would be good news. Victoria pulled her phone out, held it up, and it unlocked. Swiping, she opened the text app and read: *Hi Victoria. Sorry for the delay getting back to you. I also enjoyed my time with you and would like to see you again. Does this Saturday work?* Victoria overflowed with joy. She jumped in the hallway and clicked her heels while yelling a loud "YEAH!" Not overly sophisticated, she thought, but couldn't care less. She replaced the phone in her pocket and headed off to meet with her trainer. Time was money, after all, and she could text him later.

CHAPTER ELEVEN
Marco

The day was finally here, but Marco wasn't sure what he was feeling. After two weeks of on-again, off-again plans with Victoria, the butterflies in his stomach made him feel like it was a nervous excitement inside of him. The last time he spent with Victoria was, in his mind, a rousing success. He felt great about exposing himself and his work to her. The kiss, while especially nice, seemed a bit out of place considering it was a work meeting and not a date, per se. Nevertheless, he looked back on it with fondness. He was hoping to turn that effort into a nice contribution to his foundation by Victoria's mother, but to date, that had been more difficult than he expected. Marco felt good getting an initial meeting with Mrs. Van Hough and had hoped to close the deal by now. Unfortunately, his attempts to schedule a follow-up had been unsuccessful. Each time he called, her assistant said she was not in today or in meetings. He was getting quite frustrated. It seemed his inside track with Victoria wasn't helping. Because of that, Marco had thoughts of canceling their "date." In fact, it was originally scheduled for last weekend, but Marco asked to move it out by one week. Victoria had seemed disappointed by this schedule change, but he felt it was necessary to cool things off between them for now. The foundation would suffer if he got involved in a full-blown relationship, but lately he'd been thinking about her more and more. Would it really be that bad if they were together?

Since Marco didn't have a car, he called in a favor from the car service he used for his foundation. The plan was to pick Victoria up at her home and take her to dinner. Marco was surprised when Victoria insisted on driving to the restaurant herself. After thinking about it some, he concluded that picking her up may involve a chance encounter with her mother and create an uncomfortable mix of business and pleasure. She undoubtedly loved her mother so much that she didn't want to put her in that situation. Marco completely understood that line of thinking, as he would have done the same for his mother. In the end, the car service picked up only Marco and brought him to the restaurant where he awaited the arrival of his... he was not sure how to refer to Victoria. She was not his girlfriend, and not his client. He settled on the word "prospect." *That's it. She's my prospect*, although he was smart enough to not share that with Victoria.

It surprised Marco to see Victoria round the corner into the parking lot in yet another expensive sports car. This time she arrived in a flashy little BMW of some kind. He never needed to study fancy sports cars, so he was not familiar with this model. He watched her pull up to the valet stand, get out and get her claim ticket. She fluffed back her long blond hair, smoothed out her dress, and began walking to the front door. Marco noticed that she walked with such confidence. She owned every interaction she had with the valet and the doorman. He liked that quality in her. When he saw the valet, a young man of about nineteen, turn and look Victoria up and down like a side of beef, he noticed a bit of anger inside he didn't understand. He jumped out of the car and called out to Victoria. She turned and looked at him with her electric smile, but Marco had business to attend to first. He walked down the sidewalk and at the point where Victoria lost sight of him, Marco shot a look to the valet attendant, a look that would have caused almost certain death to most men. The valet frowned and turned away in embarrassment. Marco thought to himself, *That was satisfying*, as he turned back to Victoria and greeted her with a smile of his own. They met by the door and embraced warmly. For a second, Marco thought they would kiss again, but he diverted his head away and pulled her close in a firm hug. He was not sure if he wanted to start this night off with a kiss, so better to just not.

"It's so nice to see you again, Marco," Victoria said as they each released their hold. "It's a shame we couldn't do this last week, but I understand the importance of your work." The doorman opened the door and Marco waved for Victoria to lead the way in. She did so and took his hand as she passed, dragging him in behind her. After checking in with the hostess, they were escorted to their table. Marco learned how to be a gentleman from his father and held the chair for Victoria before she sat down. Then he pushed it in after her before taking his own seat. They ordered drinks, and the server left them in silence. Marco was a planner, and this silence didn't make him uncomfortable. He created a series of discussion topics to be used tonight. In work, as in social settings, it was important to prepare. Those were words that Marco lived by.

"It's really nice to see you again," he said to Victoria, noting how her blue dress and impeccable makeup turned her eyes a crystal blue. They were mesmerizing, and for a second, he lost his train of thought. He recovered and after a little small talk, went to his first conversation topic. "So what did you think about our last meeting?" he asked, making sure to use an open-ended question. He knew that yes-or-no questions were conversation killers.

"I had such a great time, Marco. The shopping was unexpected, but fun. The baking was great also, although I felt bad that we didn't actually finish anything. And I loved meeting all the people at the shelter. They were so nice."

As she listed off the things she enjoyed, it surprised Marco. She was excited about the baking, but not the reason they were baking. She loved meeting the people at the shelter, but not by the work he was doing there to help people. Marco didn't know what to think. The purpose of the time they spent together was to show her the work of his foundation, but she seemed to only see everything else. "I'm glad you enjoyed it all. The shopping was necessary so that your clothes didn't make you a target on the street. As you experienced, the streets can be a dangerous place."

"Oh my gosh, Marco, that's right. I was so surprised when you stood up to those guys on the street. I'm getting goose bumps now just thinking about it. You were amazing," Victoria said, and Marco noticed a softness in her voice. She reached across the table and touched his hand. The server brought their drinks, and they asked for more time to review the menu.

After they ordered, Marco took one more swing at a meaningful conversation. "So what do you think of the work being done at the shelter?" He thought he phrased the question well to get her to focus on his work and waited for the payoff.

"The children were so cute, but I felt bad for them when they escorted the man out. It was so disruptive for them," Victoria replied. Marco was getting frustrated with her answers. She was a well-educated woman, yet all she saw were the fun things. As the appetizers arrived, he attempted to collect his thoughts and reflect on how he could approach this conversation differently. It was not going anywhere.

After taking a sip of soup, Victoria wiped her mouth before breaking the silence. "Marco? Finish telling me about your father." She looked directly into his eyes again, and he felt like she was looking into his soul. Marco wasn't sure he could have been any more uncomfortable. Of all the preparing he did for tonight, this was not a question he anticipated. During their previous evening together, he had managed to tiptoe around the same conversation, stopping short of discussing the hardest part. Thankfully for Marco, she didn't press him for more, but apparently that had changed. "You were telling me about the first time your father overdosed," she continued.

Marco took a deep breath. "I wasn't planning on talking about that tonight," he said, seeing the disappointment in Victoria's face.

"I'm sorry, Marco, but I've been thinking about your dad and mine a lot lately. From what you told me, your relationship with your dad is similar to mine. I feel like we are kindred spirits in that way and I wanted to know more." Victoria's words made Marco regret shutting down the conversation and gave him the courage he needed to continue his story.

"I think the last thing I told you about was my dad's overdose when I was thirteen," Marco whispered, looking around to see if anyone else was listening to their conversation. This was exceedingly personal for him, and he didn't care to share it with anyone else. Victoria nodded and Marco continued, "He had periods where it looked like he was turning things around and then would fall back into his old habits again. It was gut-wrenching and as a young boy, I often asked myself about the role I played in his behavior. Wasn't I good enough for him? Was I doing something wrong? Why didn't he love me enough to stop?"

"That must have been heart-breaking considering how close you two were before it all started again," Victoria said in a consoling way that made him appreciate having her around to listen. These were things he had told no one else, but he felt surprisingly comfortable telling them to her.

"It was," he continued. "His bad days seemed to come more frequently than his good ones, and he was gone from home for extended periods of time. When he would come back, he begged my mom to forgive him. He always promised to change his ways, but never did. My mom had completely taken over the bakery, and my brothers, who had graduated high school by then, worked full-time with her. They hated him for leaving. Neither of them could go to college like they wanted. Their dreams were destroyed, and they always held it against him."

Marco took a breath and thought for a minute before continuing, "One time, I remember hearing my father arguing with my brothers. It sounded loud and angry. I couldn't hear exactly what they were saying, but suddenly, the back screen door flew open and the argument spilled outside. I watched from my bedroom window as it became violent." Marco remembered. In his mind he saw the picture of his brothers, one on each side of his dad. Each one taking swings at each other. The brothers easily bested their dad. He could still hear the sound of punches being landed and the sound of his mother's screams. The flashing lights appeared, lighting up everything around, and Marco closed his eyes to prevent a tear from escaping. He felt Victoria's hand grasping his, and he felt comforted by her.

"Oh, Marco. I'm so sorry," Victoria whispered as they sat in silence for a few minutes.

Their main course arrived and Victoria didn't push him any further. Marco was thankful for that. The story didn't end well, and he would rather not relive it right now. Throughout the meal, Victoria pushed her food on him and took his food off his plate. She laughed as he made a face after tasting her escargot. "Snails," he said with disgust, then laughed.

"Tell me about your plans for the foundation," Victoria said, taking Marco by surprise with the sudden subject change.

"Based on how this night started, I didn't think you were interested in talking about that," he said as Victoria burst into laughter. Marco wasn't sure why she was laughing.

"Oh, Marco, I was just playing around with you. You came in all serious and rehearsed. I was trying to lighten things up. But I am really interested," Victoria said.

Her comment surprised Marco. Was it the frosting in his

face all over again? Was he so easy to read? He was rehearsed, he admitted, but that was an admirable quality, he thought.

Talk of his foundation got him thinking about the Airstream calendar on his wall back home. He had been so conflicted lately. On the one hand, he loved the idea of expanding his foundation here. There was definitely a need, and he knew the city well. He could continue making an impact for so many people. But, on the other hand, his dream was powerful. He needed a fresh start in a new city, away from the judgment of his family and that insufferable boss of his. Although, he would miss Allison.

He noticed that Victoria was staring at him, waiting for a response. "What do you mean?" he asked sheepishly, as if he had a secret.

"Well, you are only one person, don't you want to expand? Make it bigger so you can serve more people?"

"I've thought of that, but it's so personal for me, I would never find the right people. People I can trust to do things right. People that will make the same sacrifices I make."

"What about me?" Victoria blurted out.

Marco wasn't sure he heard her correctly and replied, "What? Huh?"

"Marco, you haven't even asked about my credentials. I have a business degree from Northwestern and my MBA from the Kellogg School of Management. I would be the perfect partner for you."

Marco drained his drink and called the server over to order another one. He wasn't sure where she was going with this. In the beginning, Marco thought of her as someone who could help get a donation for his foundation. Then, after talking to her tonight, he considered that there may be something more personal for them. Now Marco didn't know where she stood. He felt like his head was going to explode. He had to think fast to buy himself more time to figure this out. "I hadn't even considered that before, Victoria. But this takes a unique set of skills that you may not have. You live in a different world than I do or the people I serve," he said, then instantly regretted the words he chose.

Before he could correct himself, Victoria responded. "So, what you are saying is that someone who lives in a gated community and wears designer clothes can't work for a foundation that helps the underserved?" Victoria asked with a challenging tone to her voice.

Marco knew that he had just stepped into something and he needed to get himself out as quickly as possible. "No, I'm not saying that. But it's really complicated for me. There are a lot of things going on that I have to consider. Can you give me a little time to think about it?"

"Absolutely. And I'm sorry that I just sprung this on you. I'm sure you think it's totally out of the blue, but I have been thinking about it for a while now," she said. "We can talk more about it later."

Marco felt that he had bought himself a little time, but he knew Victoria. She didn't wait long before circling back to subjects that interested her. She would be back.

As he finished the last of his meal, Marco ordered another drink, making his total three and three for Victoria. This was quite out of character for him. Normally he didn't drink in business settings and rarely in social ones. And given the twists and turns the night had taken, he wasn't sure which of these rules applied. Regardless, he was getting a little tipsy when he felt Victoria's foot running up and down his leg under the table. She obviously had her shoe off and seemed to enjoy herself. She looked at Marco and gave him a mischievous grin.

"What's next on your agenda?" she asked before that same grin crossed her face again.

***

They exited the restaurant and saw the driver waiting for them near the valet stand. As he helped Victoria into the car, Marco asked the driver, "Did you get my text? Is everything good with her car?"

"Yes. It will be parked in front of the restaurant when we return," the driver responded as he pulled away from the curb and headed down the road. In ten minutes, they reached their destination and pulled into a beautiful, private Japanese garden.

"I thought we could walk off our food here," Marco explained as he opened the car door to get out.

"I love this place," Victoria said. "I haven't been here for years." She took Marco's hand as he helped her out of the car. They made their way through the entrance gate and onto the walking path. The air was cool and Marco took his jacket off and draped it over Victoria's shoulders. Ahead of them was a walking path that circled a pond in the middle. There was a narrow stream that flowed from outside the garden, into the pond, and back out of the pond at the other side. The flow of water could be heard off in the distance. It was calming. There were lights strategically hidden within the landscape that illuminated the path and noteworthy plant specimens. Victoria started down the path to the right, but Marco called her back. "This is a promenade garden. It is intended to be viewed in a clockwise way down the path around the pond," Marco instructed her.

"Are you an expert on Japanese gardens?" she asked.

"No. Not really. I just like them," Marco replied, knowing it was a lie. He planned on coming here, and as he usually did, he was prepared. Marco read several publications on such things and prepared a list of interesting facts about them. Leave nothing to chance, he thought, as they started in a clockwise fashion down the path. "They sometimes call these 'strolling gardens' and people stroll from one point of interest to another." They worked their way around a bamboo screen, which revealed to them a view of the pond. "The architect put this bamboo screen here to keep you from seeing the view until the exact perfect time," he continued, educating her with his acquired knowledge. As they looked, Victoria pulled him closer and snuggled up to him. "It's beautiful," she admitted. Marco reached around her and held her back. He enjoyed feeling her next to him.

As they strolled to the next stopping point, it seemed to Marco that Victoria had more to discuss. She proved him right as they reached the next viewing point. As they came to a stop, she said, "I want to go back to the idea of a partnership."

Normally, Marco would have been thrown off his game by this sudden change of topics. Victoria frequently bounced from one thing to the next and could be shocking with her honesty and in-your-face style. But Marco found that he was getting used to her, so he was not as shocked this time. But he still didn't know where she was going with this. Marco wanted more clarity and asked, "Are you talking about personal or professional partnerships?"

Victoria responded with a simple word, "yes."

She urged them to walk on as she explained further. "Professionally, I have access to so many people who could help you and your foundation. People with the resources to change everything for you. And personally..." She collected her thoughts before continuing, "Marco, I've been waiting all my life for the right person. So many failed relationships with men who didn't want a partnership. I don't get that same feeling from you."

Marco listened intently, not sure where this would lead. He could definitely use her social status to do amazing things. But uncertainty and doubt gripped him, and after a pause, he responded, "Victoria, you don't know me. My life isn't what it seems to you. I come from a middle-class family, and I probably don't even deserve that title today." He paused again, thinking about the differences between their social standings. "I spend every penny I make on my foundation. You come from an upper-class family. We live in different worlds, and I know from experience through my foundation that these two worlds shall not meet."

"Marco, trust me. I'm not blind to the challenges we'll face both personally and professionally. And I'm not suggesting we run off and get married. I'm just asking you to consider the possibilities with an open mind."

Marco thought he promised to do that but didn't remember. His mind was racing. *I'm not sure I'm ready for this*, he thought, but her words from before were coming back to him. *Marco, you need to have meaningful, loving relationships in your life. Your foundation won't be around forever*, and he knew she was right. They would be good together, he thought. And she was smart and beautiful. So why was he so hesitant to take this step?

They enjoyed the next vista in silence, walking arm in arm. As they approached the exit, there was one last view. Marco remembered the kiss they shared and longed for another one. She was an amazing woman and an even better kisser. He couldn't believe he was admitting this, but he loved the way she felt in his arms. He was glad he initiated the first kiss they shared and would like another one. He stopped, feeling full of confidence, and turned Victoria around to face him. He looked into her eyes and she looked back at him. He wrapped his arms around her, pulled her close and felt their lips meet. He held her tight as they kissed. After several sweet moments, Marco broke off the kiss, reaching his hand up and caressing her face. He leaned forward and kissed her neck softly, and she cooed. He felt her relax in his arms.

She leaned forward and found Marco's ear and whispered, "Take me home, Marco."

Marco, without thinking, replied, "Sure, we'll have the driver take us back to your car right now." He was a little disappointed, but knew they were on the right path and could build from there.

Victoria giggled a little, and Marco wondered why. She leaned back in and whispered, "Take me to your home, Marco."

In the blink of an eye, it came back to Marco. Like a

brick striking him on the head. This was the reason he was hesitant. He couldn't bring her back to his house. He lived in a Winnebago! Just one of her cars was worth more than his house.

Everything started closing in on him, and he felt a little ill. How could he have gotten caught up in all this? *These two shall not meet*, he repeated in his head.

He didn't say no, but instead took her hand and headed to the waiting car. He wasn't sure how to break it to her that she couldn't see his house, but he knew he better think fast.

As they walked, Marco tried on a few excuses. *I'm not feeling well*, which was actually the truth. *I'm tired. I have to be up early in the morning*, he thought, and dismissed each one. They arrived at the car and he opened the door for her. Instead of getting in, she pressed forward, pinning him between her and the open car door. With Marco unable to move, she leaned in and told him, "Marco, don't worry about what I will think when we get there. I don't judge. It's you and I accept you for what and who you are... an amazing man." She put a soft kiss on his lips, then backed up and got into the car.

Marco followed while quickly making a decision that could change the course of their budding relationship. He thought, *There is no better time than tonight to find out if she's being honest.* Then he instructed the driver, "Let's head to my house."

The driver did a double take and turned around to look at Marco directly. "Did you say go to your place?" he questioned. Marco responded affirmatively, and the car lurched forward for the thirty-minute drive.

Victoria found a bottle of white wine, opening it and pouring two glasses for them. She handed one to Marco, and they toasted. "To the beginning of a beautiful, strong relationship," Victoria said. Marco gave a "salute"; they clinked glasses and took a sip. As the driver pulled the car out onto the main road, no one saw the black van that followed close behind.

***

As the limo made its way along the surface streets to Marco's house, the neighborhoods changed from beautiful downtown buildings, to working-class homes, back to the pawnshops and liquor stores. But Marco noted that Victoria didn't seem to notice. They finished their drinks as the car pulled over. "Where do you want me to let you out, Marco?" the driver asked.

"This is fine," Marco replied. He pointed to a spot across the cul-de-sac and directed him to park there and wait for them. The driver acknowledged the instructions as Marco opened the door to get out. His heart was pounding. He knew this could be either a breakthrough for them or a crushing defeat, and Marco gave either possibility an equal chance of happening. He got out of the car and extended his hand to help Victoria. She emerged from the car and Marco closed the door behind her. Marco had learned that Victoria had an excellent poker face and although he studied her intensely, she didn't have a discernable tell. She turned around 360 degrees taking in the scenery around her and Marco held his breath.

"Okay," she said. "Show me to your palace."

Marco pointed to the back corner of the cul-de-sac. He knew his house wasn't visible from the street, so they set off in that direction. The driver switched off the engine, turned the headlights off, and the sounds and sights of the neighborhood came alive. Dogs barked in several of the nearby houses, stirred by the commotion on the street. Car horns blared and sirens came and went on neighboring streets. They turned right down Marco's driveway and he felt Victoria take his hand. He hoped she didn't feel him shaking. If so, he thought, he could always blame it on the cold. As they walked down the driveway, the first motion-sensing light turned on, illuminating part of his front yard. Ten feet farther, the next light came to life, then a third. At the end of the driveway, two more lights were called to action and Marco's trailer came into full view. He waited for Victoria to drop his hand, hoping that she wouldn't. He stepped onto the stoop, fished out his keys, inserted the key, and opened the door. Although Marco wasn't planning to have a guest when he left, he was not worried about coming home to a dirty house. That would never have happened since Marco kept an impeccably clean house. His motto was *everything has a place and everything in its place.* That was at least one fewer worry as they stepped in the door and Marco switched on the light. He closed the door behind him and locked it, and for the first time, he had the courage to look at Victoria's face. He studied it intently, but had no idea what she was thinking. This made him uneasy. If she would have looked unhappy, he could at least have planned an exit strategy. But her face was expressionless.

"Show me around," she said with no inflection in her voice.

"Well, as you can see, there's not much to show you. The living room is over there," he said while waving his arm out to the right toward the couch area. He pointed straight ahead and said, "The booth is where I eat and work." Victoria stretched her neck out, appearing to look at his travel trailer calendar, but remained silent. He pointed to the small kitchen and said, "Here is my gourmet kitchen," and laughed a little. Victoria gave no response except for a slight nod.

"What's down there?" she asked, pointing down the short hallway to the left.

"It's just my bathroom and bedroom," he responded. "Nothing else."

"Let's see," she said as she leaned toward the hallway. Marco was nervous as he headed down the hallway. It was narrow, so he had to drop her hand as he walked in front of her. At the end, he opened the door, and they entered his bedroom. He switched on the light to show a queen-sized bed taking up most of the room. There was just enough of an opening for one person to walk around each side of the bed. Small storage cubbies lined the walls on both sides, filled with some of Marco's clothing. This space was spotless as well. Marco always made his bed in the morning when he got up, replacing the decorative pillows near the headboard and the duvet on the foot of the bed.

Victoria took Marco's coat off. She had been wearing it since he draped it over her shoulders at the Japanese garden. She folded it up neatly, smoothed out the wrinkles, and placed it on the foot of his bed. She turned around and walked past Marco, heading to the living area. Marco looked down at his coat and could not resist the urge. He opened the closet door, taking out a hanger. After placing the jacket neatly on the hanger, and closing the door, he followed and saw that Victoria had stopped near the front door. There was an uncomfortable pause as Marco wondered if she would open the door and walk out of his life forever. He couldn't blame her if she did. After all, how could someone who came from such profound wealth carry on a relationship with someone who lived in a Winnebago?

He looked behind him, backed up and sat down in the booth waiting for Victoria to decide. "Would you like to join me?" he asked, pointing to the bench on the other side of the table.

"Seriously?" she asked. "Nope," she replied, and Marco's heart crumbled in his chest. She looked around, but instead of leaving, she took three steps and sat down on the couch. She smiled, and Marco felt himself getting a little emotional. She patted the couch next to her and said, "Join me over here."

Marco was a little weak in the knees as he made his way to the couch, taking up the spot on the cushion next to her. "I warned you," he blurted out, wishing the words hadn't jumped out so fast.

"Yes, you did," she replied. "Marco, for this to work, we need to be completely honest with each other at all times, okay?" Marco nodded his head in agreement, and she continued, "I had a feeling it was going to be bad, but I never could have imagined this," she said and waved her arms around in front of her. "But, Marco, I know how you are. You are the kind of person who puts everything else in your life above you. That's an admirable trait, but also one that doesn't work in the long run. I told you before that you need to make time for yourself. You need a healthier balance between your work and this pitifully Spartan life you are leading. Marco, there are monks who have more than you do," she finished and giggled to herself. "And if I were you, the first thing I would do in the morning is fire your decorator. She is horrible!" They both laughed.

"But we have a lot of hours to fill between now and tomorrow morning, now get over here," she said, giving Marco her best *come hither* look. He held out his arms, and she slipped into them and they held each other. With her head on his chest, a wave of relief came over him. He couldn't ever remember having such powerful feelings for anyone. He rubbed her back and ran his fingers through her long blond hair. He could feel her breathing and loved having her close to him. He leaned back on the couch, laying his head on the pillow. He pulled her down next to him, their arms around each other, and they kissed. He alternated between kissing her lips and kissing her neck. She moaned softly as he worked his way around her neck and back to her lips. This was the first time he admitted to himself that he was falling for her. It was scary, but he really wanted to see where things led. He was finally allowing himself to envision a relationship with her, and he liked the possibilities.

CHAPTER TWELVE
Marco

"Hi, Paige. Yeah, it's me," Marco said into his cell phone while sitting at the booth in his trailer. "Is Victoria around? No, I understand… she's really busy. Just ask her to call me when she has time." Marco pushed the button to end the call and put his cell phone back on the table. It had been two weeks since he introduced her to his travel-trailer lifestyle, and things couldn't have gone better. They had shared a wonderful evening together on his couch, kissing and holding each other. He'd loved having her next to him, and had wanted it to continue. But two a.m. had come quickly and Victoria had needed to leave. Now, he missed her terribly. He went to sleep thinking about holding her and how that made him feel. The kisses they had shared. Her smile. He hadn't felt this way about anyone. Ever. Marco had tried a few times to text her, but she was extremely busy. Life was really getting in the way.

Marco picked up his phone, opened the texting app, and touched the line with Victoria's name. He read her last text. *I'm really sorry, Marco, I'm just so busy at work. We will have time together soon, I promise.* That had been three days ago.

He put his phone back down, reached up on the wall, and took the Airstream calendar down. Marco called out the name of each model as he slowly flipped through the pages. As always, he stopped at the month with his favorite model. He was so conflicted. On the one hand, he had a beautiful, smart, and fun woman in his life, and he was developing powerful feelings for her. On the other hand, his dream to move to California was strong, and Marco knew a woman like Victoria would not be willing to follow along. Her family, her business, her job were all here. Why would she? This was his dream, not hers. He shook his head as if acknowledging what he already knew.

Marco's heart skipped a beat as his phone vibrated on the table. He scooped it up, hoping to see Victoria's name show up on the screen.

Are you coming to the shelter tonight? We could really use your help. Have been missing you for the last week. —Mark. Marco's heart sunk. He had been neglecting his work at the shelter and was feeling bad about it. It was not their fault.

He replied, *Yes. See you tonight,* and put his phone back down.

He stood up and hung the calendar back up. He had things to do that he couldn't put off anymore. He walked down the hallway, getting ready to take a shower. As he opened the door to the bathroom, he thought he heard his phone vibrate on the cushion. "Don't worry, Mark. I'll be there," he said to himself and closed the door behind him. But this time, it wasn't Mark.

***

Marco enjoyed the solitude as he walked from his house to the shelter. He hadn't been there in over a week and knew he had to have his A game on when he showed up. The people of the shelter deserved the best he could give them. He opened the door to the shelter and got a warm greeting from the doorman. "Hey, Marco! Nice to see you man!" and he gave him a strong hug.

"Good to see you, too," Marco replied.

The doorman continued, "Where have you been? We've missed you here."

"Oh, you know me, saving the world," Marco replied, and flashed a smile before walking away. He was focused and ready to go. He joked with the doorman, but he was ready to change at least one life tonight. It was a busy night. He arrived a little earlier than normal, so several people were still finishing their meals at the tables. The children were running around, probably feeling a little stir-crazy as the day wound down. The noise level was quite high as their mothers scolded them and tried to redirect them into other, quieter activities.

Marco went into the kitchen, greeting the volunteers as he went. He knew most of them well. Just like Marco, they had been generously giving their time for years. As he turned around, he heard an eruption of noise coming from one table. "Hey!" A young, thin woman stood up, knocking over her chair as she headed swiftly toward Marco. When she was two steps away, it hit him.

"Andrea?" Marco said with surprise in his voice. "I can't believe it's you!"

She exploded into his arms, giving him a surprisingly powerful hug for a ninety-pound woman. She released him from her bear hug and stepped back. Marco looked down into her beaming face and said, "Let's go talk." He led her to two chairs away from most of the activity, where they sat down next to each other. Marco's heart was swelling. The last time he'd seen Andrea was at her house. He'd regretted leaving her knowing she was in an extremely unsafe situation, but he'd had no choice.

"I'm so sorry I had to leave. What happened to you?" he asked her.

"I don't blame you none. Sam would have hurt you for sure," she said, referring to her meth-addicted boyfriend. Marco looked at her as she talked. He noticed that the nervous tics and darting eyes were no longer present. Her eyes were clear and wide and her speech was coherent. He hoped she was no longer on drugs. He couldn't believe how seeing her affected him. He felt energized.

"Tell me what happened," Marco asked her. "How did you get here?"

"Well, it's thanks to you," she said, and Marco demurred. "I'm not sure why, but maybe it was lookin into Tanya's eyes and seein the hurt. But I knew I needed to do something. I needed to keep her safe. He told me he would hurt us both. Marco, I believed him." The mention of Tanya's name caused Marco to divert his gaze and look around the room in search for the cute little girl. Andrea knew what he was looking for and directed his attention to a group of children in the corner. Marco could see her big smile as she laughed and played. "I looked at them papers you left. The name of this place was on the first one, so I packed up two bags and came here. We been here for three days now. The people are wonderful and so helpful. I'm gonna get my life back together, I promise."

"Andrea, I'm so proud of you," Marco said and reached out to rub her shoulder. "The people are so helpful here. Plus, I have a few tricks up my sleeve that will help you, too."

"Thank you so much," she said, reaching forward to give Marco another warm hug.

"You have a lot of work ahead of you, Andrea, but you can do it. I have faith in you," Marco said as they released their hug. "Here is my contact number, please don't hesitate to call me if you need something. Otherwise, I'll be back in touch with you in a few days, okay?" He handed her a business card for his foundation. Andrea nodded her head in understanding, and Marco reached over and squeezed her hand before standing up and walking away. He couldn't believe his life. He got to see people change their lives for the better. No. He got to participate in helping them. He knew that it didn't always work out. Sometimes the odds were so great the people couldn't overcome them. But for the ones who did, it was a magical feeling for him.

He walked on air as he worked his way around the shelter, offering his help to the people there. Over the next few hours, Marco busied himself with worthy individuals. He made a call to help one person get a job and another call to help with housing. He gave career advice to another and provided a shoulder to cry on for a grieving woman who lost a child in a drive-by shooting. He looked down at his watch and realized it was nearly ten o'clock. They would turn the lights down soon and Marco needed to head home. He took one last lap around the shelter, saying his goodbyes before heading to the door. At the door, he fist-bumped the doorman before strolling out onto the sidewalk and into the cool, crisp fall air. This was the best he had felt in two weeks. He was making a difference again. He turned right and ran right into someone.

"Oh my God!" he said, looking up to see the person he inadvertently ran into. He was so caught up in his thoughts he wasn't looking where he was going. Finally, recognition came over his face. All he could say was a soft "What are you doing here?"

CHAPTER THIRTEEN
Victoria

Victoria's car traveled quickly down dimly lit side streets, dodging double-parked cars and potholes along the way. Her best friend, Sue, sat uncomfortably in the passenger seat. Victoria loved speed. Two days ago, Victoria had had a conversation with her, where she told Sue that she had a new man in her life. But she hadn't shared any details, so she knew Sue was excited to hear all about him. She told Sue how they met at a fundraiser, or more like how he ran into her.

"Oh my gosh, Sue. I was immediately attracted to him. Tall with looks that would make you melt. He was so handsome."

"I'm just floored by this. You never mentioned this guy to me before. Why not?"

"I just wanted to make sure it felt right. I've had so many starts and stops."

"Oh, Vic. You know I'm with you no matter how many of your mom's frogs you date."

As they continued toward their destination, Victoria told her how she'd approached him to put her number in his phone. Sue was impressed and called it epic.

"It was so cute when we were in the café and he was

telling me about his foundation. He is so dedicated to it, and I'm really impressed at how successful he has been." At the next stoplight, she reached over and pulled a few of Marco's bio-sheets he'd given her, and showed them to Sue.

"Wow. This is amazing," Sue said as she thumbed through the sheets. She read a couple of the headlines out loud. "'Military Veteran Beats Addiction.' 'Homeless Mom Turns Her Life Around.'"

"I buy coffee, Sue, but Marco is changing lives." She saved the best parts for last, describing them walking around the Japanese garden and how they kissed. Oh, the kiss. Victoria got warm inside every time she thought about Marco taking her in his muscular arms and kissing her. Sue thought they had a real, mutual attraction.

"Tell me again why you felt compelled to meet him here? Can't you just meet him out for coffee or back at his place?" She looked around, noting the deteriorating neighborhoods as they got closer to their destination.

"If I want to be a part of his life, I have to totally embrace it. I want someone who will be my partner so I have to show I can be a partner to him, too," Victoria explained.

"Vic, did he ever reply to your text?" she asked, and Victoria shook her head back and forth. "Then how do you know he will be here?"

"He's always there this day of the week. Trust me, he's the most dedicated person you will ever meet," Victoria replied, hoping that someday soon, she could introduce him to Sue. She looked at the clock on the dash and pressed the accelerator harder, knowing that her window was closing fast.

"I didn't tell you the bad part yet."

"Bad part? I thought it was all good," Sue said with a new look of concern.

"It's my mom. She's the bad part."

"What about your mom? Doesn't she approve? I thought you met him at a fundraiser."

"I did. But how do I say this?" Victoria thought for a second, then, in a screechy voice like her mother, she said, "'He's not one of us, dear. He's one of them!'"

Sue laughed an uneasy laugh. "You already know she doesn't approve of him? How will this work?" Sue asked, and Victoria knew that of all the issues they might face, that could be the most challenging one. She told Sue about her mother's warnings to stay away from Marco, but she didn't care. He was different, and she wanted to give things a try with him.

Victoria just shrugged her shoulders in reply to the question. "We'll cross that bridge when we get there, I guess."

Victoria pulled her car over to the curb and put it in park. "Okay. Let's go over the plan one more time," she said, and Sue nodded her head in acknowledgement. "I'm going to get out here. You are taking my car and will pick me up when I text you. The coordinates are in your phone," she finished.

"I'm so happy for you, Vic. He sounds amazing, and I can't wait to meet him."

They air-kissed, and Victoria got out of the car with Sue. Victoria stepped on the curb as Sue walked around the car, got behind the wheel, closed the door, and drove away. Neither woman realized Sue would be meeting him sooner than they thought.

Victoria buttoned up her coat to protect her from the cool, fall breeze, tucked her handbag under her arm, turned, and headed down the street. She never noticed the black van that pulled up to the curb behind her and switched off its lights.

As she walked down the street, she was filled with anticipation. She couldn't wait to see Marco. She was sorry she hadn't been able to see him in the past two weeks, but they both knew that life happened. Work was busy, and Marco was frequently tied up with his foundation, but she was ready for some Marco time, and she couldn't wait.

She turned the corner by the shelter and ran straight into Marco.

In an instant, the collision jolted Victoria back to reality. Her handbag went flying down the sidewalk. Marco seemed as stunned as Victoria. She caught her breath while he retrieved her handbag. Coming back, he handed it to her, and the only words he could mumble were "What are you doing here?" She expected a more positive reaction from him. Her heart was racing, but she composed herself.

"I'm sorry, Marco. I sent you a text, but you didn't respond. I told you I would wait for you here," Victoria replied, and Marco shook his head. He pulled his phone out, opened it, and saw the last text he'd received from Victoria.

"Sorry, I didn't see it," Marco replied as they both stood there staring at each other in awkward silence. Reality seemed to set in for Marco, and he began to smile. "It's been a while. So nice to see you again." He leaned forward and gave her a hug.

"Let's walk," she said, and broke the embrace before pointing them in the direction of Marco's house. Victoria saw how Marco's eyes brightened, and it made her happy. They walked in silence for the first few minutes until it was broken by Victoria.

"Marco, I want to apologize to you for how much time has passed since we got together last." Marco kept walking and didn't respond, so Victoria continued, "I'm trying to balance work and life, and don't always do it very well."

Finally, Marco found his voice and responded, "I know it took me some time to be ready for this, and I've been busy, too, but, I have to be honest, it bothered me. We had such an amazing time together that night, and I expected to see you again before now. Or at least hear from you more."

"I really am sorry, Marco. I'll do better to make time for us. It's been hard on us both. I just want you to forgive me. You told me before that your father taught you how to forgive. Am I worth your forgiveness, Marco?" she asked playfully.

Without hesitation Marco replied, "Of course you are." Victoria could tell he was being honest and the time apart bothered him, but she was relieved when Marco reached out and took her hand as they began walking again.

As they walked, Victoria returned to a conversation they'd started on their last date. She knew it made Marco a little uncomfortable, but she wanted to bring it up again.

"Back in the Japanese garden, I brought up the idea of a partnership between us. Have you given that any more thought?" She could feel Marco stiffen up at her question, and she knew this was going to be a tough conversation. But it was an important one for her.

"My foundation only has one employee."

"Allison, right? You talked about her before. Tell me about her." Victoria knew from previous conversations that Marco spoke highly of Allison, so this subject would probably put him at ease and make the bigger discussion of the topic of their partnership a little easier for him. *He may have the psychology degree, but I do pretty well myself,* she thought.

"Allison works for me. She has for the last few years. She's my assistant, but there's more to the story, and it's a long one."

"Luckily, we have time. Please tell me more."

Marco began as they continued walking, "Allison was one of the first people I helped through my foundation. She was a teenage runaway. Her father was an alcoholic, and her family life was, at times, extremely violent." Victoria began thinking about her own life as a teen. How her father protected and nurtured her. She felt safe and loved. Because of this, she had no frame of reference to understand the plight of a young runaway, but she tried as Marco continued, "When she got here, she had nowhere to go. Nothing to eat. She hooked up with a group of drug users living on the streets. She began a relationship with one of them by the name of Harry. He was fairly young, like Allison, but with no goals or ambition. He got mixed up with the group and began drinking. Unfortunately, he became an alcoholic like her dad. But he protected her, which is what bonded them together." Victoria listened intently with both fascination and sadness as they walked. *How is it we live in a society that cares so little for these people?* she wondered.

"Unfortunately, Allison ended up getting in trouble with the law. That was where I got involved. I saw something in her that was special. To be honest with you, Victoria, she's brilliant. Maybe one of the most intelligent people I know. But socially, she didn't have a clue. And in some respects, still doesn't."

"I still don't understand how a teen runaway became employed by your foundation," Victoria exclaimed.

"Well, as I said, she's quite intelligent. She picked up everything I taught her. She was like a sponge. I was drowning in the administrative goop that comes along with doing my work, and she was amazing at it. So I offered her an opportunity. We started out with a few hours a week, but it progressed to a full-time position. Over that time, I got to know her even better as a person: her likes and dislikes. She loves fashion design and wants to go to school for that. I've seen some of her designs and they seem pretty good." Victoria blurted out a small laugh, and Marco stopped walking to look at her. "What did I say that's so funny?" he asked.

"Marco. You are fantastic at your job, but fashion critique isn't exactly in your area of expertise," she said and held out her handbag. "For example, who makes my handbag?"

Marco scanned the handbag for obvious markings he might recognize but came up empty, shrugging his shoulders. "I give up," he said with a smile on his face.

"I'm sure she's good, but I would need the opinion of a professional to know for sure," she said with a laugh, replacing her handbag under her arm.

"Okay, you got me on that one. Anyway, she wanted to go to fashion school, so by working for me, I provide that opportunity. I help her put money away when she's ready to attend. Unfortunately, she is still wrapped up in several personal problems that prevent her from applying. It's a shame, really."

Victoria thought about one of her best friends who was a well-known fashion designer. "If she gets her life together, I have connections who could help her."

"Wow. That would be great," Marco said.

"We make a good team," Victoria replied, but her implication seemed to go right over Marco's head.

Victoria had enjoyed their reconnecting so much that she didn't notice the neighborhoods through which they were walking. These were tough streets. She had been here before, but always seemed too engrossed in conversation with Marco to notice. It was late and there weren't many people around. But the ones that were there were ones who welcomed trouble. Victoria's recent flashing of her expensive handbag seemed to have gotten the attention of a few locals who slowly followed behind the pair at a safe distance. They may have tired of the game. But they may not have.

They briefly stopped again and Victoria stepped in front of Marco, facing him straight on. "Thank you for sharing that with me. I know how important helping other people is to you," Victoria confessed. She moved into his arms for a hug, and Marco pulled her in tight.

They ended their embrace, held hands again, and continued their walk. They were now about a mile away from Marco's house, and Victoria shifted her thoughts to what would happen when they got there. She would welcome another night spent with him, even without intimacy. The night they'd already shared together had been wonderful. She just enjoyed being with him and in his arms.

Before they arrived, she had one last topic to discuss with him. "Marco, can I ask you about something?" she inquired.

"Of course," he responded.

"When I was in your house, I noticed a calendar with

some travel trailers on it." She thought back to that night and remembered how strange it looked on his pristine walls. "You are the most meticulous person I know, and that seemed very much out of place. So it struck me that it must have a lot of significance for you. Can you explain that? Are you going somewhere?" she asked with a sound of concern in her voice.

"It's a little late to discuss that now. It's a pretty complicated subject, Victoria, and I want to fully explain it so you understand," Marco responded. But she noticed a sudden strain in his voice, which did nothing but raise the level of curiosity and now concern in Victoria.

"I understand what you're saying, Marco, but it seems like a pretty simple answer. Are you moving somewhere or not?" she asked with an increase in the tone of her voice.

"Victoria, please," he implored, and his voice convinced her there was more than a simple explanation to the question. One that she might not be terribly excited about. Occasionally, Victoria had a stubborn streak, and it chose this time to be on full display. She deserved to know if she was wasting her time. But she recognized that by appearing to be anxious about the subject, it might make it more difficult for Marco to discuss, so she brought the volume of her voice down to a calmer level and continued to press.

"Tell me about the calendar, Marco. It seems to be important to you. Why?" she asked, changing the subject from Marco's possible relocation to something that seemed less contentious.

Marco hesitated for a minute or two before speaking, "Remember when we were talking about my father? My family and I went through those tough years when he was drinking and doing drugs. That was when he was gone for days at a time. Do you remember?" he asked, making sure Victoria was in sync with him. She nodded that she remembered. "Oh, hell... this is going to sound so stupid to you. I can't." Marco sounded defeated.

"Marco," Victoria whispered. "Remember what I said at

the Japanese garden? I don't judge. I care about you and the person you are. That's all. That's how you build a solid foundation. Please continue." Victoria was presenting her most honest self. She really didn't care what he had, didn't have, or anything else. She only cared for him, and she found herself using the word "love" for the first time. She thought she may have been in love with Marco. As much as she should have been enjoying this realization, it only added to the anxiety around his possible relocation.

"When he got clean and sober, he rededicated himself to the family and they had me," Marco said, bringing a smile to Victoria's face. "When I was seven years old, my father brought home a travel trailer and parked it in the driveway. I was so excited to see it. It was silver and the shiniest thing I had ever seen. I ran out into the driveway and my dad swept me up into his arms. He called my mom out of the house and took us both into it for a tour. It was as beautiful inside as out. I remember running up and down the hall, playing on the bed in the back, then coming to the front and playing there. At the time, I'm sure I didn't notice, but my mom didn't share my or my dad's joy. Voices were raised, and an argument started. I heard glass break when I was in the bedroom and I remember quietly closing the door and sitting on the bed, listening as things got louder and louder. After what seemed like forever, I heard more glass breaking, then the door to the trailer slammed closed. I heard footsteps coming back and felt relief when my father opened the door. He laid down on the bed with me and the next thing I know, I woke up in my bed.

"The trailer seemed to be a constant source of fighting between my mom and dad. My dad had a dream to see the country, and the best way according to him was to take his family in a travel trailer. In looking back now, it didn't seem like a good idea since my brothers and sister were already teens and not interested in being squeezed into a tiny trailer. Mom didn't like the idea, either, since they could never get time away from the bakery to travel. So to them, the trailer represented the ongoing failure of my father. It got moved to the backyard where it fell into disrepair. For me, it represented something completely different."

"It became your dream, too, didn't it?" Victoria asked.

"Yes, it did. Shortly after moving it into the backyard, Dad ran an electrical cord to it to provide power. We would sit in the booth and he would tell me fantastic stories about trips we would someday take together. He would show me pictures of the Grand Canyon and say, 'Son, we'll go here someday, I promise.'"

"It never happened, did it?" Victoria gently asked.

"No. Over the years, the trailer became a home for bugs, rodents, and animals. My dad and I stopped meeting out there," Marco continued. "Shortly after he passed away, my mom had it towed away and scrapped. I was too young to do anything about it. Besides, my mom seemed so relieved to have it gone."

Victoria's inner voice was telling her to go *there*, So she did. With an intentional softness to her voice, she asked, "So tell me how this story of the trailer and your calendar relates to you leaving?"

Marco took a deep breath and said, "First, Victoria, please know that my plans are not intended to hurt you. It's something I have wanted to do for several years now. The fact that I met you and have feelings for you only complicates things." Victoria heard him say he had feelings for her, and her spirits perked up a bit. *Surely he's not going to leave me after admitting that*, she thought.

Marco blurted out, "I started the process of buying a new trailer. My plan is to take it on the road for about a year before permanently resettling my foundation in California."

It took a second for his words to register with Victoria. When they did, it was like a punch to her gut. She felt all the wind leave her. All she could muster was, "You're leaving me?"

Marco pleaded with her, "No, Victoria. I'm not leaving you. I'm just leaving, that's all."

This explanation didn't make Victoria happy, and her voice got louder. "Keep your foundation here, Marco. You're already established. People know you. Why start over in a place where you aren't known?"

"I'm sorry, Victoria, but you don't understand," Marco responded, but his words only hit her harder and she continued to get more upset.

"Go and find yourself. Take your year off and go find whatever you are looking for. Leave your foundation here and after you get this bug out of your system, come back. I'll be here for you, I promise," Victoria pleaded.

"You think I'm lost?" Marco retorted with a caustic tone. "Are you trying to save poor me? The lost soul? Trust me, Victoria, I'm not lost and I don't need you to save me!"

As the disagreement escalated, the small band of locals who'd taken notice of Victoria's handbag had grown in number. It was around a half-dozen people now, and they were closing in fast.

"I'm not saying you are lost," Victoria said, trying to calm everything down. "I know why you want to take your trip, but I don't understand why you can't come back here. Let me help you with your foundation while you are gone."

"What do you know about running a nonprofit?" Marco asked with significant skepticism.

"Nothing," she admitted. "But you taught Allison, and you can teach me. I want to learn. We can do it together."

Victoria's words were interrupted by the sounds of a deep male voice. "What do we have going on here? A lover's spat? Cute." As he finished, Victoria looked around to see a circle form around her and Marco. She looked at the men and they appeared to be exceptionally rough. Each one wore oversized clothing that was torn and dirty. Two of them carried improvised weapons: a long board and a metal pipe. They appeared to mean business, and Victoria thought they might be in trouble. Her heart raced, she was sweating, and her mouth went dry. She didn't know what to do except to look to Marco for support. He tried to move to her side but was cut off by two of the men.

Without warning, they punched Marco in the stomach, and Victoria cried out, "Marco!" Before she could get to him, her path was cut off by two of the other hoodlums who pushed her to the ground. She landed hard on her backside and lost her breath, falling backward until the back of her head hit the grass behind her. She saw stars.

"What do you want?" Marco asked breathlessly, bent over at the waist. From her vantage point on the ground, she watched the ringleader walk over to the curb. He bent down and picked up Victoria's handbag where it must have landed when they pushed her to the ground. "Well, this is a good start," he said as he held it up to examine it. "Nice!" He looked down at Victoria and asked, "What is it? Chanel?" And let out a bellowing laugh.

Victoria snorted, "It's Fendi, you moron," and all the men broke out into laughter. They all took turns telling the man, "She schooled you, boss!"

After they had their fun, the boss yelled at them to shut up, then refocused on Victoria and continued, "Sorry, princess. I'm not up-to-date on my brands," and gave Victoria a toothy grin. "What I know is that if someone like you is carrying it, then it's pretty special." He tried opening it and said, "Let's see what she has inside." This made Victoria angry, and she tried to get up to get her possessions back. Before she could get up, she felt her legs being swept out from under her and she crashed back to the ground with a thud. He continued to focus on her.

"Don't make me hurt you, princess. Because I will if you push me." He finished by moving his jacket to the side, revealing something that Victoria thought was a handgun, but she couldn't be sure. Her body was aching from the falls and she just wanted this to be over.

One of the other men chimed in, "Hey, boss, lover boy has a watch."

This got his attention, and he walked over to Marco, holding out his hand. "Let's have it, Romeo." Marco didn't hesitate to take it off and give it to the man. He held it up to the light and examined it carefully. He turned it over and over in his hands, then held it out as if to judge its weight. The boss walked over to Victoria and addressed her. "It's a cheap knockoff. A piece of crap. Loverboy over there is pretty cheap. He's trying to impress you with a crappy knockoff watch," and again, he broke out into robust laughter. He walked to the street, wound up, and threw it against the curb. Victoria shielded her eyes in case any of the pieces ricocheted her way. "Impressive, huh?" He directed his comments toward Victoria. She knew that it was best to say nothing.

Marco addressed the men, "Just take what you want and leave us alone."

The boss responded, "Don't worry, Romeo, we will. But I'm not sure you're gonna get off quite that easy. We have something special in store for you."

The words struck dread in Victoria. She was in fear for both of their safety but had no idea what to do. The boss pushed his jacket aside again and walked over to Marco. With one continuous motion, he removed the item from his waistband and used it to strike Marco on the side of the head. He crumpled to the ground and laid there motionless.

"No!" Victoria yelled and tried to stand again, accepting whatever was going to happen to her. She wasn't going down without a fight. Suddenly, she heard squealing tires, and when she turned to look, she saw the doors of a black van open, allowing four men to pour out. They headed in her direction with lightning speed. One of the men moved over to her and scooped her up while the other ones focused their efforts on the hoodlums. As the man carried her away, she fought unsuccessfully to get loose. They headed back to the mysterious black van, but Victoria caught glimpses of the action she was leaving behind. It was a free-for-all. Punches thrown and landed by the newcomers while the hoodlums appeared to have taken significant damage. Victoria continued fighting the man carrying her as he made his way toward the black van. She landed the toe of her shoe squarely in the man's groin and he cried out in pain. To Victoria's dismay, he didn't put her down, but continued until he got to the van. The man handed the still-battling Victoria to the driver, who pushed her into the back of the van with a shove. She turned around to see the other men pile into the van. The last man in closed the door, and the tires squealed as they headed down the street. As they turned the corner, Victoria saw a police car driving in the opposite direction at a rapid speed with its lights flashing and siren blaring. She closed her eyes and prayed they were heading in Marco's direction.

Victoria had no idea what was happening. She was terrified, and as she bounced around in the back of the van, she asked several times, "Where are you taking me?" No one would answer her. Finally, when the hulk-sized man in the passenger seat turned around, Victoria recognized him from some security work her mother had contracted recently, and it all hit her. This was the work of her mother! But how? Victoria knew it wouldn't do any good to ask anyone in the van. They were all being paid handsomely, she was sure, and with that came the expectation that they would keep their mouths shut. As they neared her estate, the man in the passenger seat sent out a text as they turned the corner and rolled up the driveway. The engine idled as the compound gate swung open with a squeak and a clang. Once clear of the gates, the tires squealed again, and they proceeded down the driveway and into the circle drive in front of the house. The van had hardly come to a complete stop before one of the men slid the door open. None of the men would look at her as they waited for her to exit the vehicle. Once clear, the tires squealed again, and the van sped away. Victoria headed for the house and was almost to the front door when she realized she had no way to unlock it. Her keys were lost along with her handbag. "Damn it," she said, but her time outside would be minimal. Before she could reach to test the door handle, it swung open for her to enter. As she walked in, she didn't have to look and see who let her in. Helen's perfume gave it away.

CHAPTER FOURTEEN
Victoria

Victoria opened her eyes but was afraid to move. Last night, or more accurately, early this morning, when she finally got to bed, she was already feeling the effects of the rough treatment she received at the hands of those social rejects. Unfortunately, she was roughed up some by the men from the van as well. Now, just moving her toes, elicited a pain response that traveled up to her brain. Victoria turned her head and looked over to the nightstand next to the bed, thankful to see her cell phone resting there. Fortunately, she had stored it in a pocket, otherwise it would have suffered the same fate as her handbag and keys. She gave the command to her phone and told it to call Helen, unsure if it would.

She was relieved to know that even with a cracked screen, it seemed to still be working. After two rings, a voice came over the line, "Yes, Ms. Victoria. What can I do for you?"

"Can you bring me some Advil, Helen?" Victoria croaked, using the least amount of energy and movement she could.

"Yes, ma'am, I'll be right up." The line went dead and Victoria closed her eyes again and drifted off. She thought about last night and still couldn't believe what had happened. She replayed some of the events in her mind. Everything was going along so well between her and Marco. They were talking and enjoying each other's company. Then it all went bad. *Where did those degenerates come from?* she wondered. Before she could answer, there was a knock at her door. "Come in," she said.

The door opened, and it was, as expected, Helen, her mother's most trusted staff member, carrying a tray with a glass of water and a small silver dish with two tablets on it. Helen was dressed in her uniform that was spotless and perfectly pressed. Her hair was impeccable. She ran the house and had been here for as long as Victoria could remember. Helen knew where all the family bones were buried, and Victoria was quite sure that she already knew what happened last night. But as they say, *Loose lips sink ships*, so Victoria knew that Helen would never admit it. She placed the items on the bedside table and asked, "Can I get you anything else, Ms. Victoria?"

"No. Thank you, Helen."

Helen took the tray and headed to the door. She opened it, but before she left, turned back toward Victoria. "Oh, Ms. Victoria? Your mother asked me to tell you that when you get up, she would like to see you in the library."

She knew better than to show emotion with Helen. Otherwise it would get reported back to her mother and that was the last thing she wanted. She ignored Helen and kept her eyes closed until she heard the door click behind her. *Damn her.* Victoria slowly sat up in bed and her fears were confirmed. Every muscle in her body seemed to be crying out at this simple effort. She reached over, took the pills, and returned the items to the nightstand. Her mind switched gears from her pain to think about Marco. Victoria was worried sick about him. Once home, she had been determined to take her car and return to Marco to make sure he was okay. But by the time she got home, her body had told her otherwise. She had been physically not able to return so she'd tried calling him. No answer. After only two attempts, her mental exhaustion and deteriorating physical condition had left her no alternative and she had fallen into a deep sleep.

With pain racking her body, she reached for her phone and unlocked it. Her heart sank when she didn't see any missed calls or texts from Marco. "Where are you?" she said to no one. She selected his contact information and sent him a text. *Where are you? Are you okay? PLEASE CALL ME.* She dialed his number, but it went directly to voice mail. She'd already left him two messages, so she decided to just hang up.

Now that her head was clearing, she remembered that during the night, she had been awakened by the ringing of her cell phone. She'd hoped it was Marco, but it had been Sue instead. Victoria remembered that they'd had plans for Sue to pick Victoria up at Marco's house. Sue was checking in because she hadn't heard from her. Victoria hadn't been able to explain everything but had begged her to go to Marco's house and check on him. Now, she didn't remember hearing back from her, so she went through her phone, frantically looking for some communication from her. She saw a voice mail and listened to it.

"Vic, I just left Marco's... umm... house? I think I have the right place. I don't think anyone is here. I knocked on the door pretty loud, but no one answered. There's no car in the driveway, either, so I don't think he's here. I didn't want to make too much racket. This is a really sketchy neighborhood, Vic... I'm worried about you. Call me back when you get this message and let me know what's going on, okay?"

"Ugh," Victoria said as she began to ease her way out of bed and sat on the edge. Her head was spinning from everything that was going on now. To top it off, she had to deal with her mother, too. She sighed. Her mother could be difficult to deal with. She was incredibly passive-aggressive. But she was also intelligent and sneaky. Victoria had to be at her best when dealing with her, but today, she was far from it. *More like a failure*, she thought, but her mother would not be put off for long. She would have lots to say when Victoria got down there.

She stood up, testing her strength and balance and was surprised as she managed to start walking across the room. She was still sore, but it was tolerable. She looked down and saw a six-inch bruise on the side of her leg. "Crap, no short skirts for a while," she said. "At least it's fall," and mustered a brief smile. She walked into her dressing room, selected a pair of black yoga pants and a large hooded sweatshirt. She dressed and moved to the mirror to check out the damage. She looked at her face straight on, then turned to the right and back to the left doing a full survey. "All things considered, not too bad."

Victoria had two more pieces of business to attend to before going to face off with her mother. She took her phone and dialed Marco's number first. It never rang and again went straight into his voice mail. *Crap*. After listening to the greeting, she decided to leave another message. "Marco, please call me and let me know you are okay. I'm worried sick about you," she said and hung up the phone. She dialed the phone again and it rang.

"Hello?" a woman's voice answered.

"Sue, it's Victoria..." she said but was quickly cut off by her friend.

"Vic... what the hell is going on with you? Are you okay?" she asked frantically.

"Honestly, Sue, I'm fine, but I need another favor. Can you go back to Marco's house and see if he's there yet? I'm worried sick about him and haven't been able to get in touch with him all night."

"Of course, but what's going on? And I still have your car," she said with great concern in her voice.

"Don't worry about the car. Just go check on Marco and I'll fill you in later. Text me when you get there to let me know what you find," she said.

"Okay. I'll let you know. Love you, girl," she said before ending the call.

Victoria had done all she could. Now to jump from the frying pan into her mother's fire.

***

Victoria stood outside the library door collecting her thoughts. She needed to stay calm and collected when talking to her mother or her mother would eat her alive. Suddenly she heard a voice from inside the office say, "Come on in, dear. I won't bite." It was the sound of her mother's voice and it was like nails on a chalkboard. *How the hell does she know I'm out here?* she thought. She gritted her teeth and walked around the corner. Her mother was sitting in her chair reading the newspaper as usual.

Before Victoria could even sit down, her mother said, "Helen, can you get us some tea?" and she heard the "Yes, ma'am" from some unknown corner of the house. She was starting to dislike this house more and more. Victoria gingerly took a seat next to her mother who didn't look up from her paper. Both were content to play the waiting game. This was high-stakes poker for Victoria and she didn't want to show her cards. Helen came back with a silver serving tray, two china cups of tea and all the accessories. As she put the tray on the table between them, she said, "Ms. Victoria, I brought you some of those cookies you like. I hope you are feeling better." Helen smiled, then turned to make her way out of the room and Victoria noted again whose side she was on. Victoria reached for a cup and fixed her tea and continued to wait it out. Finally, her mother neatly folded her paper and slid it along her chair, then reached out and fixed her own cup of tea. She sat back in her chair and turned her attention to Victoria. *Here we go,* Victoria thought as her mother began to speak.

"So how was your night, dear?" she opened with, knowing the answer already. "I went to bed early and didn't hear you come in." Victoria's face started to flush already, seeing where this was going.

"Really, Mother? You're doing this again? I'm pretty sure you know exactly where I was and when I got home," Victoria snorted, "and for the record, I'm not at all pleased."

Mrs. Van Hough calmly took another sip of tea without diverting her gaze from Victoria. "I'm sorry that Mommy cares about you so much, dear," she said sarcastically. "It seems to me that you weren't able to keep yourself safe, so I had to do it for you."

"So hiring your security goons is your way of showing you care?" Victoria replied, and her mother shrugged her shoulders and said, "You can't argue with the result."

"So how long have you been spying on me?" Victoria asked, choosing to jump right to the heart of the matter for her. "I'm sure this wasn't the first night you had the boys following me."

"Oh, honey. You're my only daughter. You can't blame me for wanting to make sure you are okay. But that's really not the issue, now, is it?" she said causing Victoria to have a quizzical look on her face. "You really don't know? Oh my. You're such an intelligent young woman, I'm sure you know." She set her cup down and appeared to collect her thoughts. "The real issue is him."

The reality finally hit home for Victoria and she fired back, "He has a name. It's Marco."

"Well, *he* needs to find someone from his own social class. I've told you before, Victoria, he isn't one of us."

Victoria was in full defense mode. "What do you know about him and his social class?"

Mrs. Van Hough exhaled and sat back in the chair. She reached down next to her chair and retrieved several file folders. She opened one of the folders and took out several eight by ten black-and-white pictures, orienting them properly toward Victoria, then sliding them across the coffee table. She motioned for Victoria to take a look. Hesitantly, she picked them up and looked at the first one.

It was a picture of Marco and Victoria in the coffee shop the day they met for their first date. The depth of her mother's surveillance was clear from this first picture. She put the first one on the table and examined the second picture. It was one of her and Marco going into the back door of the restaurant. The third caught the two of them in an embrace and the last showed Marco coming out of his house. Victoria flipped them onto the table in disgust. Mrs. Van Hough fished out the one in front of Marco's house and pointed to the trailer. "I especially like this one," she said, continuing with her sarcastic tone. "Victoria, dear, you cannot be serious about this," she said as her finger tapped on the trailer. "Look around you. We have this," she said, waving her arms around. "He has this," returning her finger to his trailer.

"Marco is an amazingly thoughtful, unselfish, and giving person. He's not like any of the other more 'suitable' men you want me to date," she said, making air quotes around the word "suitable." "He was raised in a loving home and taught how to be a good man. A good partner."

Her mother opened the top folder and took some papers out. She reached down on the table, retrieving her readers and putting them on. Victoria cringed with the thought of what was to come. "Let's see here... Marco DeFranco, born of Italian immigrant parents. Baker by trade, running a small bakery on the south side. His father was an alcoholic and a drug addict who died from an overdose when he was a teen. You should see the toxicology report that shows what was in his system. It's pretty impressive," she said and turned the paper around showing an official-looking document. Victoria fought to contain her anger. *How can she reduce the loving relationship Marco had with his father to a toxicology report?* she thought.

"Among the other wonderful traits Marco has, he's extremely honest with me. We spend a lot of time talking about his relationship with his father and I share details of my relationship with my father. We both had very loving relationships in spite of our fathers' faults. There's no new news here, Mother," Victoria continued, finding that she was raising her voice a little. She noticed that her response caused her mother to bristle and she made the connection between her comments regarding her dad and her mother's reaction. Her mother hated that Victoria thought of her father with fondness and had done everything she could to spoil that. Her spirits were raised slightly knowing that she touched a nerve, so she continued making the case for Marco. "He runs a successful foundation helping a lot of people. You would know this if you took the time to open your eyes," Victoria said, challenging her mother's perspective of Marco.

Before her mother could continue prosecuting her case against him, Victoria felt her cell phone vibrate as it made her designated sound indicating she just received a text. Normally, she respected her mother enough to not interrupt their discussion by checking her phone, but not this time. She fished her phone out of her pocket and unlocked it as her mother slapped down the file folders onto her lap in disapproval. "Victoria, this is not acceptable!" she said as Victoria waved her concerns away with the flick of her hand. She was surprised how good it felt knowing she was standing up for herself, but the feeling quickly faded as she saw the text was from Sue and not Marco. Still, she knew it could contain good news so she opened it with great anticipation. It read: *I'm here at Marco's house. I knocked on the door several times, but no one came to the door. I'm sorry. I'll stick around for a few minutes and see if you want me to do anything else. Let me know.* Victoria felt tears welling up in her eyes and she fought to contain them in the presence of her mother. She wondered how much more she could take, but knew her mother wasn't finished. Without responding, she turned her phone off and replaced it in her pocket, returning her attention to her mother.

Mrs. Van Hough slowly shook her head and sighed again and Victoria knew she had more cards left to play. She steeled herself for the next round. "Victoria, please. I take no pleasure in this. I'm only trying to open your eyes to reality. Do I need to continue?" A tear rolled out of Victoria's eye and down her cheek before she could wipe it away. Her mother saw but didn't acknowledge her emotions.

After a brief moment of silence her mother began to tab through the remaining folders on her lap. She settled on one in the middle of the stack and opened it. "Let's talk about his foundation, Victoria. As I told you before, he has one employee and has no office space. We spend more money maintaining this compound than he brought in last year in donations. And let's not forget his salary of just over $36,000 for last year."

"He chooses to not take a big salary. He wants to keep that money in the foundation," Victoria told her mother with satisfaction.

"No, dear. That's the salary he earned from his day job," her mother continued. Up to this point, none of her mother's intelligence had surprised Victoria. Marco had been honest with her and she with him. But talk of a day job confused Victoria and the look showed clearly on her face. Before she could conceal it, her mother picked up on it. "Ahhhh..." she said with a smile starting to form on her face. "You don't know." She fished through the pages in the folder, finding the one she wanted. She turned it around so Victoria could see. It was a picture of Marco that looked like a work ID photo. Under it, the words *Social Services Bureau* were written in bold letters. "He's a social worker, Victoria. Didn't he tell you that?" Victoria tried to maintain a neutral expression but had already shown her hand. She was having a hard time keeping her composure, and more tears were escaping her eyes than she could wipe away with the sleeve of her hoodie.

"Victoria, let's just get down to the bottom line on this. He's not one of us. He doesn't belong here and he doesn't deserve you. I'm asking you, as your mother, to stop seeing him immediately."

Victoria was near the breaking point and could only say, "No... I... won't stop. We have feelings..."

"I was hoping you would have come to your senses, but apparently not," her mother continued, going in for the kill. "I'm not asking you to stop seeing him, I'm telling you."

Victoria stood up and started to leave the room. Her mother, for the first time, began to raise her voice. "I control everything, Victoria! Your job, your finances, your life! You would be well advised to listen to me."

As she went around the corner, she couldn't hold back the tears anymore. They came flowing freely down her face as she made her way back to the safety of her bedroom suite. The pain had returned to her body, making things even worse. As she ascended the stairs, she heard another text come through her phone. She stopped midway up and quickly pulled out her phone. She saw a new text from Sue and swiped to open it. *Vic, we have a problem. I was looking in Marco's windows and saw what looked like blood on the floor. So I got into the trailer. Don't ask me how... but I found him on his bed. It looks like a crime scene in here.* Victoria sat down on the stairs and sobbed. She wasn't sure why, but she did, and she didn't care who saw her.

CHAPTER FIFTEEN
Marco

Marco finally knew what people meant when they said they felt like they've been hit by a truck. It took a few minutes of him lying in a pool of his own blood to realize where he was. It was all starting to come back to him: the fight with Victoria, the men, and then darkness. Then the pain. He was on his side, so he pulled his legs under him and tried to get to his knees. He opened his eyes, or at least the one good one on the right. Marco's left eye was swollen shut and there was dried blood and grass on the left side of his head and face.

He was dizzy and having a difficult time focusing his one good eye. Looking around he saw that, at least right now, he was alone on the street. Slowly he began to rise to his feet, but as he got close, he lost his balance and fell back to the ground with a thud. He was near a bus bench so he crawled the five feet until he could grasp it for support. The second try was the charm and Marco was back on his feet, although rather unsteadily. He checked his watch to see the time and realized it was missing. "Damn," he said as he tried reaching into his jacket pocket to get his cell phone out. He soon realized that his jacket was gone, along with his cellphone. Marco wanted desperately to call Victoria and see if she was okay but couldn't. He shook his head in disbelief but stopped as the pain felt like a spike in his head. Luckily, he only had a few blocks to get to his house so he started in the proper direction. How could it get any worse, he thought, then took two steps and realized his shoes were gone as well. "Anything else?" he asked and looked up toward the dark sky.

The last thing he remembered was when the leader of the thugs came over to him, then everything went dark. He had no idea what could have happened to Victoria. His heart ached thinking about it. Marco stopped to look around the immediate area for evidence of Victoria's fate. He saw signs of multiple scuffles and hoped that she had reached deep down within herself and was able to fight off these dangerous men. Down the street about ten feet, he saw her handbag, which seemed strange to him. *Why wouldn't they have taken it with them?* he thought as he got to it and reached down, picking it up. The handbag was a mess. It was torn, scuffed, and empty. Someone cleaned it out. He saw one of her shoes and fought his mind, which wanted to go to a dark place with thoughts of Victoria's demise. He made his way covering the twenty feet to her shoe and picked it up. A careful, one-eyed examination provided no clues to Victoria's condition or whereabouts. He wanted to cry, but every part of his body hurt too much and all he could think about was getting home.

As he started to walk again, his frustration continued to build. He felt responsible for all this. If he had just hired someone to drive them home, it wouldn't have happened. Now, any chance he had to build something with Victoria was lost.

Slowly... painfully he worked his way the four blocks to his home. Without stopping, he continued down the driveway as the first motion light fired. The brightness caused him to cover his eye. He paused for a minute, shifted Victoria's damaged handbag and shoe to his left hand, and felt around in his pockets to find his house key. He sighed when the realization hit him that his keys were in his jacket. But even in this heavily compromised state, Marco knew how much of a planner he was. Not even the smallest details went unaddressed by him and the possibility of him not having a key was one of the scenarios for which he had a solution. Although, this would be the first time he had put this plan into action.

He continued down the driveway, past the security lights and the front door, shuffling his way to the end of the trailer and around to the back. Once there, Marco saw the lone window leading to his bedroom. He leaned down, turning over an empty flowerpot to reveal a screwdriver. He took the screwdriver and wedged it between the window and the frame. With significant effort, Marco heard a pop and the window opened. He left this window unlocked for just such an event. He only had to crawl in now and he was home free.

He reached down and moved the flowerpot closer to the trailer, stepping on it to start the process of squeezing his body through the window. On the inside of the trailer, against the wall, was a dresser and Marco hoped to use that dresser to help get him inside. In spite of all Marco's planning, he didn't account for having limited flexibility and only one eye when performing this difficult maneuver. Slowly he inched his frame through the window, across the dresser top until the edge of the bed was just inches from his reach. He stretched and could touch the comforter with the tips of his fingers. One last reach and the palm of his hand was on the bed. Suddenly, the bed shifted and any support Marco had was now gone. Like a sack of flour, Marco's body headed for the floor. As his feet followed, they swept everything that was on top of his dresser with him. Picture frames, decorative vases, and bottles of cologne all went crashing to the floor along with Marco. The first thing to make contact with a solid surface was Marco's bad eye, followed by the rest of his body and finally his legs.

As he lay on the floor, Marco felt new pain he hadn't felt

before and it was excruciating. He touched his face and felt blood pouring out of a new injury he sustained from the fall. All he cared about was getting into bed. If he could get there and sleep it all off, he would be fine, he thought. Willing his legs to work, he pulled them up underneath him and lifted his body off the floor. He reached forward across the bed and crawled slowly onto it, leaving a snail trail of glass, dirt, and blood along the way. When his head reached the pillow, all motion stopped and Marco's lights went out.

***

Crunch, crunch... Glass was breaking under someone's feet. Marco heard the commotion in his house, but he was too weak to do or say anything. "Oh my God..." he heard someone say. The voice belonged to a woman, but he didn't recognize it.

"Come on... come on... answer your phone," the woman said to herself. "Vic! Thank God you answered. Wait... are you crying? Is everything okay?" the woman asked. She was talking on her phone, so Marco could only hear her half of the conversation. "Okay, okay, calm down... I'm actually in his house... Yeah... I had to crawl in an open window... Vic, he's here on the bed, but there is blood everywhere." She whispered, "I can see he's still breathing, but it's like a crime scene in here. There's glass and blood everywhere. Vic, his head looks pretty beat-up. I'm afraid..."

Marco tried to find his voice. His first attempt brought no response from his vocal cords. His second try elicited a barely audible squeak. Marco's third try finally brought a word. "Victoria..." He waited for a response but got none. He tried again, and this time had more success. "Victoria!"

"Oh my God... he's calling your name," the unknown woman said. "Okay, hang on." She bent down to Marco and asked, "Marco, can you hear me? My name is Sue. I'm friends with Victoria. She's worried sick about you. Can you hear me?"

All Marco could muster was, "Victoria!"

"Okay," Sue replied into the phone. "I'll try." She reached down and held her phone against Marco's exposed ear and yelled, "Go ahead, Vic."

Marco heard a voice in the phone. "Marco, honey, are you there? Please say something. Are you okay? We're getting you help. Hang on."

Marco heard her but could only muster three words in response. "I'm so sorry."

The sound of sirens roared in the background, and he could hear Sue saying, "They're here. I'll call you in a few minutes. Okay. Love you, too. Bye."

Sue leaned down and said into Marco's ear, "Help is coming, Marco. Hang on."

In spite of all the pain he was in, Marco knew Victoria was safe, and that was all that mattered to him. A tear ran down from his one good eye.

CHAPTER SIXTEEN
Victoria

"Hi. Can you tell me what room Marco DeFranco is in?" Victoria asked the woman behind the information desk.

After consulting her computer, she replied, "He's in room seven-oh-six. The elevator is over there. Take that to the seventh floor." She pointed over Victoria's shoulder in the direction she needed to go. Victoria thanked the woman and headed toward the elevator.

So many things filled Victoria's head as she walked. The last time she saw Marco, he'd been lying on the ground in a heap. She knew he was badly injured based on what Sue had told her. She'd described his bedroom as a crime scene, so Victoria was very unsure of what she would see. On top of that, she had learned the disturbing information that her mother was involved in the attack. She wasn't sure to what level, but the fact that she was involved was too much for her to reconcile. She'd spent a lot of time thinking about it over the past two days, and had decided that it was best to tell Marco everything she knew, even if it meant exposing her mother.

The elevator door opened, and she stepped on and pressed seven. As the elevator ascended, so did Victoria's anxiety. What would Marco think? Would he even want to continue their relationship knowing how extreme her mother's actions were? The thought of not being with him left an empty hole inside of her, and she wanted to cry. The doors opened, and she stepped out into the hallway, turning left, following the signs to room 706. At the door, she paused, then opened it slowly, peeking her head inside the room. Her heart sank as she saw Marco lying in the bed. She could see IV bags hanging by the bedside and a monitor above the bed. The monitor showed what looked like his heartbeat. Seeing Marco like this was worse than she expected, and tears began to stream down her cheeks. She stepped into the room and cleaned off her face before continuing to his bedside. She pulled a chair over and sat down next to him in silence.

Marco stirred in the bed, and she reached out to hold his hand. She examined his face, but couldn't tell the extent of the damage because of the snowy white bandages covering his left eye and much of his face. She had a feeling it was bad but was glad that she couldn't see for herself. He opened his other eye, looking around the room before landing on Victoria. He squinted as if he wasn't sure if she was real.

"Victoria? Is that really you?" he asked.

"It's me, Marco. I'm so sorry this happened to you." Her voice started to break up with emotion, and a tear ran down her cheek. Marco reached out and tried to wipe it away, but even that limited effort caused him to withdraw in pain.

"Why are you crying? It's not your fault. You didn't do this."

His comments caused her heart to sink, knowing it was not entirely true. She didn't say anything, while trying to figure out how to open the conversation.

"How are you feeling?" she asked, and reached out to touch the bandages on his head. He winced at the slightest contact. "Oh, I'm sorry."

"I'm just really sore. Lots of pain."

"What are the doctors saying about your recovery?"

"There shouldn't be any permanent damage. I was worried about my eye, but they said my full vision will return. It'll just take some time," he said with a sound of exhaustion in his voice.

"I'm glad to hear that," she said.

Victoria was hoping he would have been in better shape to have this discussion, but it appeared that he wasn't. Regardless, it had to happen today. She had to leave tomorrow on an emergency extended work trip and didn't want to disclose the information to him over the phone. She was worried about how he would react, but it was important that she tell him.

"Marco, I need to tell you what happened after those guys hit you in the head." He nodded, indicating that she should continue.

"After they hit you, a van pulled up and several men got out. I saw them coming, but I wasn't sure what was happening. They beat up several of the thugs. The others ran off." Marco looked away as she revealed the details. He seemed to be in pain, but Victoria wasn't sure if it was pain from the injury or the pain of remembrance. Either way, it was bad.

"I don't understand. Who were the men?" Marco asked slowly as he focused back on Victoria.

"They were members of a security detail my mother has used for other things. They have been following us since the beginning."

"Your mother? Your mother is behind this?"

"No, Marco. No. Not all of it," she said as she stood up and walked over to the window. "Maybe... I don't know."

"Did she have anything to do with the men who beat me up?" The possibilities seemed to dawn on him. "Did your mother pay someone to beat me up?"

She returned from the window, pleading, "No, Marco! She wouldn't do that." But she really didn't know the answer herself.

"How do you know?"

Victoria lowered her head. "I guess I don't. I hope my mother wasn't involved in that, but I'm just not sure, Marco. I'm sorry."

"What happened next?"

"After they beat up the thugs, they carried me to a van and brought me back to my house."

"I'm glad you made it home safely," he said. "But they left me on the ground. They didn't know if I was alive or dead." Victoria's heart broke as he recounted such an important and unfortunate detail. "How did you find this out?"

"I figured it out in the van, but my mother confirmed it for me yesterday."

"So, over smoked salmon and mimosas she dropped this on you?"

"No. Marco... I don't know what to say." Thinking back to her conversation with her mother, Victoria felt a large pit form in her stomach. She truly didn't know the level of her mother's involvement. Were her mother's thugs just at the right place at the right time, or was there more to it? The way her mother had told her didn't give her any clue either way. She was certainly very smug and self-satisfied, but that didn't mean she'd paid hoodlums to beat up Marco. Victoria was so confused.

The door opened, and a nurse came into the room. "Time for your pain medication, Mr. DeFranco," she announced. After drawing the medication into a syringe, she pushed it into his IV, then left the room. The silence was deafening, and it concerned Victoria.

After a few minutes, Marco finally said, "Victoria... I just don't know... where we... go from... here." His words were long, and his pronunciation was unusual. "This... sounds like something... we won't be... able to overcome."

"No, Marco. We will get through it. I promise," she said with determination. "Marco?" There was no response. She leaned over him and listened closely. The sound of his breathing made her feel better. Then he began to quietly snore. "I'm so sorry, Marco. Please don't give up on us," she said, before kissing him gently on his forehead between the bandages.

She left with a feeling of defeat overwhelming her. For the first time, her normally self-confident self began to wonder if they were going to be able to get past this.

CHAPTER SEVENTEEN
Marco

"Is that me?" he said out loud. Marco looked in the mirror and shook his head. He raised his hand and traced the cut on the left side of his face with his fingers. Sometimes he didn't recognize himself. The stitches were still in place and the cut was tender to touch. Half his face was a wild mix of colors. Marco pointed to the darker area of bruising around his eyes and said, "What a beautiful tanzanite blue." He ran his index finger to the outer edge of the damage and said, "It's a marvelous canary topaz." He thought for a minute before saying, "No, it looks more like a yellow diamond." He smiled a half smile, satisfied that his mind still contained some gemology information he studied for previous fundraisers. When you were around wealthy people, it paid to be able to recognize their gem selections and compliment them by name. In a mocking voice, he said, "My, Mrs. Smith, that's a lovely red beryl. Have you been to the Wah Wah Mountains before?"

It had been a week and a half since neighborhood thugs had played lights out on his face. After three days in the hospital and three more recovering at home, Marco still wasn't feeling like himself. But the game must go on. Without him, the foundation didn't exist. That meant the people he spent the last five years helping would have been pushed back into the gutter with no hope of reaching any of the scraps that fell off society's table. He couldn't let that happen.

His freshly pressed tuxedo was a head-turning contrast to the damage on his face. Marco wondered how he would be received by the donors at the fundraiser tonight. But he had no choice. Tonight was the granddaddy of them all, and Marco would be there. He was hoping to collect some scraps of his own from the wealthy attendees and had spent his time this week, between headaches and medicated naps, preparing for the event.

Through one of his contacts, he got a copy of the guest list and put the knowledge to good use. He was familiar with most of the names on the list and had interactions with some of them. A few even donated to his foundation. He hoped to increase the names on his donation list by two or three tonight. "If my face doesn't scare them off, that is," he said, and reminded himself that he still needed to come up with a white lie to tell the attendees tonight. Saying, "I got beat up by a street thug," wouldn't play well with the social elite.

A horn sounded in the driveway and Marco knew his ride had arrived. He gathered his new cell phone, put it in his inside jacket pocket, and put his keys in his pants pocket. He turned all the lights off, locked the front door, and exited his trailer. The short walk to the limo tired him out, and he was reminded how deconditioned he was from his week off. "This should be interesting," he said as he got in the back seat. He greeted the driver, and they backed out of the driveway.

Marco sat back, closing his eyes and reflecting. His life of a week ago was so different from today. Last week, he'd had a job as a social worker. A job that, admittedly, Marco had disliked, but it had paid the bills. While in the hospital, of all places, he'd received a visitor from human resources. They were predictably apologetic at seeing him in the hospital, but they weren't having any luck contacting him. Marco still didn't know how they found him, but they did. His attendance record was the stated reason, and they had already gotten approval from the union. There would be severance, but not much. They thanked him for his service. At first Marco was upset. *I'm in the hospital and I just got fired*, he said to himself. But after giving it some thought, he considered it a blessing disguised as an HR rep. With that decision made for him, he sped up his plans for moving out of town. After what he had been through, he was more motivated than ever to leave.

His biggest complication, the only fly in the ointment, was Victoria. He'd never expected to have feelings for her, but here they were. The night of the attack, they had a vigorous discussion about Marco's plans. Up to that point, he hadn't found the need to disclose them to her. When he did, Victoria didn't warm to them. In fact, she'd said some things he felt were rude and unjust. It reminded Marco how he felt with his family when they questioned his plans and motives. They never understood him and never would.

Then, although the visit seemed fuzzy in his mind, he thought about Victoria's trip to the hospital. It had been good to see her, but the news she'd brought was disturbing, to say the least. To think that her mother might have had something to do with him getting beat up was almost unimaginable. Was she that evil? Or was she just trying to watch out for her daughter? Marco had only met her three times briefly, so it was hard to determine with any level of confidence what her motivation was. He had to consider the very real possibility that she had orchestrated the entire event. That frightened him. For the past several years, Marco has walked the most dangerous streets in the city, somewhat fearful of those who inhabited them. Now he had to digest the possibility that his near demise had actually come from the uppermost levels of society. The irony, and concern, had caused him many sleepless nights.

The revelations regarding her mother left his and

Victoria's relationship in chaos. Over the past week, he and Victoria had played phone tag, but had never really spoken. Truth be told, Marco was probably trying to avoid speaking with her. He didn't know what to say and wasn't sure where they should go from here. He wasn't even sure there was a path for a viable relationship with her. Fortunately for Marco, Victoria had to go on a last-minute work trip to Peru. The remoteness of her destination made communication difficult, so he could avoid the tough conversations that would be necessary if they were going to try and move their relationship forward. In the end, Marco wasn't sure they would help anyway. He was moving, and nothing was going to stop him. Now with his job gone, moving would be even easier. In one respect, he was glad he never had to expose that job to her, but part of him felt like he committed a lie by omission and he wasn't proud of himself for doing it. Nevertheless, she didn't know, so problem solved.

The limo sped down the surface streets toward his destination, and Marco used the last few minutes of the trip to make up a story about his injuries. *It must be believable*, he thought, and elicit a response of either respect or sympathy from the donors. *I crashed my Mercedes? I was sitting courtside at the basketball game and a player ran into me?* Nothing he tried seemed to fit the bill. Marco was a planner, so trying to come up with something on the fly would not do. Finally, he thought, *I ran into a burning building to rescue someone and I got hit in the head by falling debris. Hmmm*, Marco thought. That could work and kicked it around more. Many of his potential donors had deep contacts in law enforcement or in the fire department, but he doubted they would take time to check out his story. The car pulled up to his destination and Marco realized he was out of time. Despite his intense need for preparation, he would have to make some details up as he went. Marco thanked the driver, stepping out of the limo and closing the door. He looked around and frowned. It was not the entrance he wanted to make, but he had no choice.

This fundraiser was being held in one of the most prestigious brownstones in the city. Built in 1870, it was the crown jewel of the neighborhood. Within its four magnificent stories it had its characteristic brown stone façade, wide front steps leading to the stoop, and ornate carvings. It was impeccably restored in 1994 at a cost estimated to be around five million dollars, although no one knew exactly.

Unfortunately for Marco, he wasn't able to appreciate the beauty of the façade. Nor would he have had the pleasure of walking up the wide, beautiful stairs. He was in an alley behind the building. His normal contact who guarded the front door wasn't working tonight, so he had to go with plan B. Regardless, Marco always found a way and he walked down the alley and up to the back door. He noted the time, then knocked lightly. Before dropping his arm, he admired his new wristwatch. *Yeah, it's a knockoff, but a damn good one*, he said to himself. The door opened and a young man peered out through the crack in the door. "Right on time," he said, and opened the door just enough for Marco to enter. He stepped in as the young man closed and locked the door behind him. "Good to see you again, Marco," he said, and the men hugged warmly.

"Thanks for the favor," Marco said and handed the man an envelope that Marco prepared the night before.

"I would do anything for you, Marco. You helped me, big-time. But this will come in handy for sure," the man said as he folded the envelope and placed it in his pocket.

He gestured toward a hall, and Marco set off through the back section of the house. He heard voices and saw staff members moving in and out of the kitchen doors to his right. Some carried trays into the kitchen for refills, others carried trays out overloaded with delicious and expensive foods. The smells assaulted Marco's nose. *What is that?* he thought and determined it to be a nasty mix of food, old house, colognes, and perfumes, and it made his stomach do a flip. As he walked, he noticed the staff members looking at him and pointing, and they reminded him of the facial damage he wore. He was certain to get the same reaction when he entered the main entertaining space.

As he passed the kitchen, he fell in line behind a tall young lady carrying a loaded-down serving tray. She strained to support its weight. He followed her down the hall as she opened the door and entered the main entertaining room. Two more staff members attempted to enter the hallway, and Marco skillfully navigated between them, emerging unnoticed. He had never been in this house, so he took a few minutes to look around. His preparations included educating himself on the brownstone style of home typical in this part of the city, but the pictures didn't do this home justice. The room was exquisitely decorated with period furnishing, original dark wood floors, and beautiful trim work around all the doors and windows. Marco was impressed by the craftsmanship. The eleven-foot ceilings helped keep the noise down to a dull roar and Marco saw that, as usual, it was full of the city's elite members of society. He remembered his guest list and began taking an inventory of the attendees he recognized. *Fred Grimes and his wife, Ella. He is the chief of neurosurgery at the biggest hospital in the city*, he reminded himself. *Eldridge Fox, who is an incredibly successful investment banker, is here, too, but not with his wife.* Marco recently read that he lost her to cancer after almost sixty years together.

He moved from one room to the next, taking additional notes of the occupants. *Alexandra Warford, not here with her husband.* He laughed. *Who is that? Some new arm candy. Sarah Fitzgerald, old money. Inherited.* He noticed the lights were dim, and he considered he might escape without many people noticing his face. Now if he could have just gotten a check or two, it would have been a successful night.

In the front parlor, he heard the sounds of a string quartet and as he entered, he saw Jerry Couch near the front window. Jerry was the CEO of a large manufacturer with headquarters in the city. He knew Jerry from previous conversations but had never convinced him to make a donation. Yet.

He approached Jerry on his left side to prevent him from seeing his mangled mug. Jerry was looking at what appeared to be some kind of literature about the renovation of the house. *Jackpot*, Marco thought as he waited for his moment. "Beautiful house, isn't it?" he said, only turning his face slightly toward Jerry.

Jerry took a minute or two to stop reading before he responded. It felt like an eternity. The wealthy liked to make you wait, Marco thought. It was a power thing. "It certainly is," he said and turned back to his brochure.

"Those stairs and the stoop are beautiful and an important part of the architecture," Marco said, not feeling a good vibe yet.

Without looking up from his brochure, Jerry replied dryly, "Okay. Dazzle me with your knowledge. I can't wait to hear." Marco realized things were not starting off well, but it was too late to abort. He had no choice but to continue to wade into the shark-infested waters. As he got ready for nights like this, Marco prepared bites of knowledge ranging from minor things to interesting facts. His best information he normally used to try to save a conversation, but he needed saving right from the start, so he played his trump card first.

"Well, the most common explanation for the steps and the high stoop relates to the horses at the time. Apparently, they piled horse excrement onto vacant lots around the city. Large piles of it." Marco held his arm up to his shoulder height to give him a visual. "When it rained, there was an excrement river that flowed through the streets. The high stoop provided refuge from the rather foul-smelling river," Marco concluded and waited for a reaction. That little factoid sure sounded better when he rehearsed it in his kitchen this morning. Now, Marco was not so sure, but he waited.

Finally, Jerry replied, "It's like being up shit creek without a paddle, huh?" and let out a bellowing laugh, amused by his quick-thinking response. Without looking at Marco he said, "Funny, right?" And continued laughing. When Marco didn't respond, Jerry finally turned and looked. Suddenly, the laughter stopped. Jerry craned his neck farther as if trying to see around Marco, but Marco knew what had Jerry's attention. "What the heck happened to you?" he asked. "Did you get hit trying to get on a city bus?" He now had his full attention aimed at Marco.

Just like that, and without even trying, Marco had him. Although, he never intended for his injury to be one of the subjects for the night. Nevertheless, Marco welcomed the switch from their awkward first exchange and now saw a chance to redeem himself. He quickly regrouped to remember the story he fleshed out in the car.

"Well, I was out for a walk the other night. I couldn't sleep after working several late nights in a row at my foundation. We help people who are desolate and have nowhere else to turn." Marco paused, letting the information register with Jerry. "As I was walking, I noticed smoke coming from the front porch of a neighbor's home. I ran to the front to investigate when suddenly—" Before Marco could continue, he felt a hand on his shoulder. He stopped and looked down at the meat cleaver resting there. He turned his head and looked directly at the shoulder of the person who so rudely interrupted. As his gaze moved skyward, he realized this had to be one of the biggest men he had ever seen. His anger was softened somewhat, knowing this man could squash him like a bug.

"I'm sorry to bother you, but can I have a word in private?" the mountain said while gesturing to an empty corner near the front door.

"Sure," Marco said and apologized to Mr. Couch, promising to return in a minute. As they walked, Marco's thoughts turned from curiosity to excitement to dread in the few seconds it took to reach their destination. He had never seen this man before and couldn't imagine why he wanted to talk. Would he be unceremoniously removed from the event? He had no idea. They stopped in the corner and Marco faced the unknown man. "What can I do for you?" he asked and steeled himself for an unpleasant answer.

"Are you Marco DeFranco?" he asked, but Marco was sure he already knew he had his man. Marco nodded his head in acknowledgment. "Excellent. I have someone who is especially interested in talking with you."

Initially, Marco was curious, but his street smarts quickly kicked in and he got nervous. This was all too strange, he thought, as his throat went dry and his heart raced. Who even knew he was here? he wondered. "I don't normally go off with strangers. My mother taught me about stranger danger. Who wants to see me and regarding what?" Marco was satisfied with his fast thinking and believed he had the upper hand in this chess match. He stood a little taller now.

"Mr. DeFranco, I was under the impression you treat people better than this. Do you really want to keep such an important patron waiting? We're wasting time, sir."

Patron. It wasn't a word he had used before, but he liked it. Patron of the arts, patron of science, patron Marco, patron of hope. He realized he had to see who this patron was, so he nodded his head in agreement before saying, "Let's go."

The man turned around and headed away, and it surprised Marco to see him ascending the first step to the second level before turning to make sure Marco was following. The man turned back around and continued up the stairs with Marco in tow. As they continued ascending the stairs, Marco realized how much quieter it was getting. He also noticed how much the stairs creaked under the man's weight and he began having second thoughts. They reached the top of the stairs for the second floor and Marco's concerns grew stronger when they didn't stop, instead heading up the next set of stairs to the third floor. With each step, his dread grew, and he wondered if they had played him. But who would have been interested in hurting him? he wondered. He had no enemies. At least not ones who could have afforded to arrange a rendezvous on the top floor of a multimillion-dollar brownstone mansion. They reached the top of the stairs and the mountain stopped moving. He pointed to the last door down the hall and said, "Your patron is waiting for you there."

Marco noticed the beads of sweat beginning to form on his forehead. He took a handkerchief out of his pocket and wiped them away, knowing they would soon be back. He took one step forward before the mountain stepped behind him, blocking the stairs and any hope of an easy or timely escape. Marco turned around and looked. Even one step down, the man was still far taller than Marco. "You are wasting time, Mr. DeFranco," he said and pointed to the door again.

Marco turned toward the door and his date with destiny. It felt as though his feet were in quicksand as he attempted to take the first step. Slowly, he moved. One step at a time, like a convict on death row. He waited for the mountain to yell, "Dead man walking!"

After what seemed like an eternity, Marco covered the ground to appear in front of the door. He raised his hand and timidly knocked on the door.

"Go in, Mr. DeFranco! You are expected!" came the mountain's voice behind him, which caused Marco to flinch. Marco reached out and put his now sweaty hand around the knob and turned it. The door opened with surprising ease and Marco entered the room where he would have an encounter that could change his life forever.

CHAPTER EIGHTEEN
Marco

As the door swung open, Marco took stock of the room revealed before him. It was set up as a well-appointed office with an enormous mahogany desk in the middle, two high-back chairs in front, and two serious-looking men flanking the desk. Marco noted they were almost as big as the mountain who escorted him here. Behind the desk was a chair, but the chair was turned toward the windows at the back of the room, obscuring the occupant from sight. Marco took a step from the hallway carpet to the hardwood floors and they creaked, making him aware of the complete silence in the room. A voice came from behind the desk and without turning around said, "Please come in, Mr. DeFranco. We have something to discuss."

With some hesitation, Marco slunk toward the desk. Each step brought another squeak to the otherwise silent room. He stopped between the chairs and waited. After what felt like an eternity, the mystery person said, "Gene, can you please leave us alone? Hal, you can stay for now." With that, one of her twin gargoyles walked to the door, exited the room, and closed the door behind him. Marco heard a lighter click and saw smoke rise from the chair. Finally, its occupant turned around to reveal herself.

It surprised Marco to see who had summoned him there. After what Victoria had revealed about the night he'd been beaten up, seeing her sitting there caused a chill to run down his spine. Although her methods were rather unorthodox, she'd brought him here for a reason. Marco was determined to understand why.

"Mrs. Van Hough. How nice to see you tonight," Marco said, greeting her with a forced smile. She took a drag from her cigarette and eyed Marco with what looked like contempt before blowing the smoke in his direction. Marco was well versed in the social customs of the wealthy and tested the temperature of the room. Without an invitation, Marco moved in front of a high-backed chair and took a seat. The reaction he received was exactly what he'd expected.

Mrs. Van Hough leaned forward, and in a stern voice, she said, "Mr. DeFranco, there is no need to get comfortable. This meeting won't last long." Another chill ran down his spine as it became clear that this was not a social call.

She lived off intimidation, but Marco needed to present a strong front in response. He crossed his legs, displaying a lack of concern. *Community college psychology. Check*, he thought.

She took another drag from her cigarette, stubbed it out, and continued, "You don't understand why you're here, do you?"

Marco paused before responding, then replied, "I have an idea that it has something to do with your daughter." He raised the stakes by continuing, "As you know, she's in Peru, but I'm pretty sure I can get her on a call and we can all talk about this." He reached in his jacket pocket and as he did, the remaining gargoyle turned toward him, brushing his suit coat aside like a Western gunslinger, revealing what appeared to be the grip of a handgun. Marco recoiled from the dreadfully fresh memory of his recent brush with just such a weapon. The meeting was taking on a far more serious tone to Marco.

Mrs. Van Hough quickly said, "Relax, Hal. Mr. DeFranco doesn't even have a permit to carry." Hal moved his jacket back to conceal his weapon as Marco dragged out his phone, not realizing why since he no longer had any intention of calling Victoria. He extended his arm with his cell phone, but in a flash, it was gone. Hal the gargoyle, with lightning-fast reflexes, had snatched it from his hand. He gave Marco a smile as he slipped it into the breast pocket of his coat.

Mrs. Van Hough slowly shook her head back and forth. "Do you know why Victoria is in Peru?" Marco wondered if this was a trick question, then realized there will be many land mines placed for him during this interaction. He remained quiet. "Because I sent her there." She looked at Marco for a hint of understanding and apparently didn't get it. "I felt it was of supreme importance that we meet alone tonight. Before things progress any farther." Marco knew she went to great measures to have this audience with him. Alone. She sighed loudly, and Marco thought she had lost her patience with him already. What was he missing? he wondered. "Let's get to the heart of the matter, shall we?" she said, and it relieved Marco that this conversation was moving along. "It appears that my daughter, Victoria, is smitten with you, and although I don't know why, she remains steadfast in her insistence on continuing a relationship with you. I'm here to tell you that will not happen."

In the silence that sunk back over the room, Marco thought about her admission. Without input from Victoria, he had made several assumptions about their fledgling relationship. The most central of his beliefs was that although Victoria's mother was probably not happy that Marco wasn't a member of the upper crust, she was holding her nose because her daughter's happiness was most important. The rest of his relationship assumptions were based on this. Now Marco saw that he had built a house of cards that was ready to fall at any moment. The last kick to the cards was remembering the mugging. Victoria's words came back to him. The men in the van took her to safety and left him there. Her mother was not okay with the relationship, and he wondered why he hadn't seen that before.

"I'm not sure what that has to do with you," Marco said, gathering enough courage to stand tall against her. "Victoria is old enough to make up her own mind." Marco knew this would probably push her button. He was right. Mrs. Van Hough stood up and slowly walked around the desk until she was standing directly in front of Marco. She leaned down. Her face was now inches from his. The smell of smoke and alcohol on her breath as it combined with her perfume made him feel queasy. She took her hand and cupped his chin. Her hold on him went from grandmotherly to vise. She knew it hurt, but he resisted the urge to cry out in pain. She took his face and turned it, examining the damage.

"You have an interesting way of doing makeup, Mr. DeFranco," she said with a gleeful sound in her voice. She released her grip and leaned back on the front edge of the desk. "May I ask what happened?"

"I was out walking last weekend when I came on a home with smoke coming out." He stopped mid-sentence when he sensed he had just stepped into a trap. His fears were confirmed when she broke into laughter. It was a disturbing cackle that sounded serious and evil, and his confidence sank.

"Save your breath, Mr. DeFranco!" she said, now with force in her voice. "Don't you think I know what happened?" Fear gripped Marco as the words came out of her mouth. He'd known she had played a role in the attack, but hearing it straight from her took things to a completely different level. He began to shake a little and hoped she didn't notice.

Without exposing his hand, he asked, "Did you have

something to do with the attack?" There was trepidation in his voice that he couldn't hide.

"Mr. DeFranco, do you think I would do something like that?" she asked with a smile that went from ear to ear. Based on what Victoria told him, Marco knew the answer was yes. He was seeing how ruthless she could be. She was wealthy, with many friends, and he concluded that she should not be underestimated.

"You endangered your daughter's safety to keep us apart!" he said, but only half-heartedly. Before the words could settle, he watched Mrs. Van Hough's frightening transformation from stern woman to monster. She leaned into him again and her bony fingers reclaimed their grip on his damaged face.

"You are the one who endangered my daughter!" she screamed now in a full rage. "You took her to those dangerous places where she didn't belong!" Her grip increased on his face and he flinched from the pain. "You are not one of us! This will not happen, Mr. DeFranco. Do we understand each other?" Her rage eased slightly and Marco shook his face out of her grip.

"Oh, I understand," Marco said, marshaling a small amount of defiance. "I understand that I don't have to stay here and listen to this." He attempted to stand, but her rage was back.

"Sit down!" she yelled as Hal put his hands on Marco's shoulders and forced him back into the chair. He landed with a thud, bottoming out in the chair and sending jarring pain up Marco's spine. She walked around the desk and sat back down in the chair. She picked up a cigarette case, taking one out and lighting it. She took a deep drag. Hal's hands were still on Marco's shoulders and Marco pushed them away.

"Mr. DeFranco. You need to understand your place. You bring nothing to the relationship. You don't deserve my daughter," she said with contempt. Marco saw she was calming down. "You must know that I can make life in this city impossible for you. Let's not let things get to that point." Marco knew these weren't empty words.

Mrs. Van Hough reached down next to her chair and produced a file folder. She said, "I know everything about you: your finances, your childhood, pity about your father." Her words stung. "Oh, I'm so sorry you lost your job. I'm sure you found tremendous fulfillment working there. It's a shame how they did it, in the hospital and all."

A pit formed in Marco's stomach as she revealed the extent of her knowledge. He had developed strong feelings for Victoria, but he didn't see a way to overcome such a ferocious obstacle like her. She took the folder, handed it to Hal the goon who handed it to Marco. Marco opened it and saw the first thing inside was a photograph of him lying on the ground unconscious. His face was in the dirt. It was too much for him to absorb, so he flipped to the next one. It was a picture of him leaving his trailer and the next one was of him leaving his old job. He fanned through the documents and saw copies of his financial statements. He was astounded at the depth of her research and her ability to get protected items. To say that Marco was concerned would be an enormous understatement. It terrified him.

After giving Marco time to look through the folder, she continued, "Now, Marco. Can I call you Marco?" He nodded his agreement. "I consider myself to be a fair woman. I'm asking something of you and I don't expect you to do it without getting something in return." She waved at Hal and he snatched the folder from Marco's hands, handing it back to Mrs. Van Hough. She replaced that one along the side of the desk and pulled out another. It made its way to Marco via the goon exchange. "I'm prepared to make a substantial donation to your foundation, a life-changing donation, if you agree to never contact my daughter again. Take a look," she said and waved her hand toward the folder.

Marco opened the folder and found a document, and behind it, a cashier's check. He pulled it out and examined it. There were more zeros on it than he had ever seen on a check in his life.

"I think you will agree that I'm being quite generous," she said. "This is a onetime offer that expires when you walk out that door. I suggest you sign the document inside and take the money." Marco removed the document and scanned it. He couldn't believe he was even considering it, but what choice did he have? She could make life a living hell. Hal reached into his pocket and retrieved an ink pen, handing it to Marco. Conflict filled him as he considered his options. Could he move forward without trying to work things out with Victoria? The money certainly was life-changing. With the money, he could fulfill all his dreams. But they would be without Victoria.

"Marco, I'm a busy woman, and it's getting late. Sign the form and let's move on with our lives," she said. Marco took the paper out of the folder, signed it, and handed it to Hal, who passed it to Mrs. Van Hough. Once complete, he returned his gaze to Marco, holding his big mitt out in front of Marco's face. Marco took the pen, opened his jacket, and placed it deliberately into the pocket. This annoyed Hal, who shook his hand repeatedly at Marco.

"Hal! I'll buy you a new one as your Christmas bonus! Please show Mr. DeFranco to the door," Mrs. Van Hough scolded. With that, Hal dropped his hand. Marco was having immediate second thoughts about taking the money. Sensing that, Hal reached under Marco's left arm and forcefully pulled him to his feet. "Good day, Mr. DeFranco," Mrs. Van Hough said as she turned her chair toward the windows.

Marco tucked the folder under his arm and headed toward the door. He was immediately overcome with emotions, many of which he didn't understand. Is this what betrayal felt like? He never remembered having experienced this before but thought that was partly it. He identified a feeling of profound sadness, too. He needed time to process all this. The office door closed behind him as he headed down the stairs to the ground floor. He was having a hard time maintaining his composure and wanted to cry. Luckily it was dark in here, he thought. Tears welled up in his eyes as he exited the house, through the front door this time. He stopped on the curb and reached into his pocket to pull out his cell phone to call the driver. He patted all his pockets before realizing it wasn't there. He began walking down the sidewalk as his tears fell like rain.

CHAPTER NINETEEN
Marco

This must be what it was like when a tornado struck, Marco thought. It seemed like they always hit places where people live in trailers like him. He was by nature an exceedingly organized person. *Everything has a place and everything in its place.* But today's activities were straining his ability to deal with clutter and disorganization. Moving day was coming soon and Marco was neck-deep in preparations. Boxes were piled waist-high everywhere. He couldn't understand where all this stuff was coming from. He built yet another box, sat on the floor in the living room, and began removing items from the storage compartments under the couch.

His new cell phone rang. It was now his third one, and he hoped he could keep this one a little longer than the last two. He crawled on his hands and knees to the banquette to see who was calling. It was his mother. Normally he wouldn't be overly excited to answer. She was a little pushy and had a way of making him feel guilty about everything. But today, she should have important news for him, so he answered the call with anticipation.

"Hi, Mom. What did you find out?" Marco blurted out.

"Patatino! I don't speak to you for weeks and this is what I get from my youngest?" Her Italian accent was still thick, even after all these years. "Can't I get even a little small talk? Maybe I'm sick or dying. How would you know?"

"Okay, Mom. I'm sorry. How are you?"

"That's better. You need to treat your mother better. I went to the doctor this week. He called me obese! Can you believe it, pasticcino? I told him, 'You realize I work in a bakery, right? I have to sample my goods.' Anyway, I still have that pain."

Marco took the phone away from his ear and waved it around while she talked to the air. Mom liked to review all of her aches and pains each time they talked, but Marco wasn't in the mood to listen. After a few minutes, he put the phone back to his ear. "... and my leg is still bothering me, but your brothers help me a lot. Are you there?"

"Yes, Mom. I'm listening, but I'm trying to pack, too. Can you tell me what you found out, please?"

"Okay," she said with a sigh. She had more pains to discuss, but Marco wasn't in the mood to hear about them. His mention of packing got her off on another tangent. "Speaking of packing, I still can't believe you are leaving your mother. Don't you love me?"

"Mom, of course I love you, but I have to live my life. We have been over this a dozen times. Now can you tell me what you found out?"

"Mio Dio, your mother will never see you again," she said before finally getting to the information Marco wanted to hear. "Well, your brothers have agreed. I wish it wasn't this way, but if it's what you want."

Marco's spirits soared with the news. "Oh my God! Really? They agreed?"

"Yes. The paperwork is with your uncle Mario. You should hear from him tomorrow. So when are you leaving me?"

"Oh, Mom. I'll come and see you, don't worry," Marco said as the front door opened. Allison walked in and Marco used her arrival as an excuse for getting off the phone. "Allison is here, Mom. I have to go."

"Marco, you need to marry that sweet girl—"

"Love you, Mom!" he said as he ended the call.

Allison closed the door behind her, put her handbag on the table, and sat across from Marco. He didn't normally notice or comment on fashion things, but he was trying to make Allison feel better. After all, when he left, so did her job. "New handbag?" he asked.

"Oh, Marco. You don't care about fashion. It's not on your list of fundraiser study topics," she said. "But to answer your question, yes, it's new. But it's not real. Someday I'll be able to afford one. But school first." Marco knew there wasn't any contempt in her words, but he still felt guilty for moving and putting her out of work. She had been a loyal employee for several years, although he still couldn't remember exactly how many. "So when do you pick up the thing?" She pointed up to where the calendar was. But it was missing off the wall.

"It's called an Airstream and I pick it up in two days. I can't wait to get all this stuff put away. How do people live like this?" he asked and spread his arms out in a sweeping motion pointing to all the clutter.

"Really, Marco? Look at these boxes." In typical Marco fashion, all the boxes were the same size, aligned in perfect columns with labels that detailed the contents of each box.

Marco changed the subject away from his little idiosyncrasies. "Thanks for coming over. I have something I want to tell you. When I pick up my Airstream, I'm coming back here, loading up my belongings. and hitting the road."

"So soon? Why the hurry?"

"I need to move on. I'm ready and the timing is right." As he finished, his phone vibrated and Victoria's voice could be heard saying, "Hi, Marco!" He made this text notification of her voice several weeks ago. When he heard her, it made him smile.

"You glow when you hear her voice, Marco."

Normally, Marco would have argued with her about her observations, but in this case, he thought she was right. He had loved his time with Victoria, but he couldn't ignore the elephant in the room. Her mother was rich and well connected and made her wishes known. He had to take her threats seriously, which ironically helped push him into deciding to leave. He hadn't talked to Victoria since then, and he felt guilty. He had powerful feelings for her, but things were stacking up against them. He opened his phone and read the text. *Hi Marco. I really miss hearing your voice, but I understand that you are really busy. I just wanted to let you know that I'm thinking about you and I can't wait to see you again.* This text made Marco feel even worse. He didn't know how to tell her he was leaving, so he was just going. Some would have called him a coward, but he didn't think so. It would be less painful this way for them both. Besides, how would he have been able to tell her that her mother made threats against him?

"Earth to Marco, come in Marco," Allison said, and Marco snapped out of his daze to look at her.

"Sorry. I have a lot on my mind these days," he admitted. "Hand me that folder on the table please," he said, pointing to the banquette table. Allison retrieved the file folder and handed it to Marco.

"So mysterious. What 'cha got in there?"

"I feel so bad about leaving you without a job," he said as he pulled a piece of paper from the folder. "I spoke to several people on your behalf. Anyone on this list will hire you tomorrow. You have your choice. I made sure they know how lucky they would be to have you." He handed her the paper.

"Marco, that's so nice of you. Thank you." She had a smile on her face. "I hope you didn't tell them how much I make. Or don't make," she said with a tease. "Although, they couldn't pay me any less or it would be called a volunteer position." Marco laughed uneasily. Was he really taking advantage of her all this time? He didn't think so, especially considering the next thing he gave her.

Marco pulled the next sheet of paper from the folder. "I

have something else for you." He handed it to her and waited for her reaction.

"What is this? A bank statement?" She scanned the document but couldn't figure out its significance. He saw the confusion on her face, so he stood up next to her.

Marco pointed to the top of the document. "During the first year we worked together, I got to know you. Your passion for fashion design was so strong. I know you want to go to school and study fashion, but you don't have the money. Well, each month, I put some money away for you and didn't tell you about it. This will get you closer to your dream, Allison."

"Marco! Oh my God!" She jumped around like her legs had springs in them. In mid-spring, she hugged Marco, then continued springing again between the stacks of boxes and back around to where Marco was standing. "This is the best day ever!"

"I have one more thing to give you, Allison," he said as the springing ended. He pulled out the last two pieces of paper and handed them to her.

"This looks like a title document. It has the address of your house on it. What is this?"

"It's all yours, Allison. I'm giving it to you. It's not much, but it's all yours. Well, in two days," he said, quickly correcting himself. Allison was overcome and said nothing; she sat down on the bench.

After a few minutes of looking at the documents in silence, Allison said, "Marco, I don't know what to say. This is so generous of you. I feel bad."

Her reaction surprised Marco. "Why do you feel bad? This is a good thing."

"You have spent the last five years of your life doing things for everyone else and no one does anything for you, including me."

He sat down across from her. "Allison, you have given me so much. I get friendship, compassion, hard work, and a little dose of attitude from you. I feel rewarded nearly every day for knowing and working with you. I wish I could do more for you."

"I'm blown away. Thank you so much. I don't have any fancy gifts for you, Marco, but I have something. Advice."

Allison was extremely opinionated, and he knew he wouldn't be able to escape without a heaping helping of Allison's life advice. She had great insight into human behavior and was the first one who recognized that Victoria had feelings for him, long before he did. At times, it had been a source of tension between them, but in the end, she was right. Here she went again.

"Marco, I saw the light in your eyes when you received that text. So I'm pretty sure it was her. But instead of responding, I saw you close your phone and lock off your heart. I could sense the pain and conflict it was causing. You aren't taking her with you, are you?"

These comments surprised Marco. Her insight was uncanny, and it made him uneasy. He didn't like knowing he could be read so easily. "It's complicated," he said in almost a half whisper.

"That's a cop-out. There's nothing complicated about it. Take her with you or you will regret it forever. Trust me."

Deep down, he knew she was right, but it would not happen. He made up his mind. Despite what his heart was telling him, he was going it alone.

CHAPTER TWENTY
Victoria

Whoever coined the phrase *tickling the ivories* had no idea how to play a handcrafted musical instrument. From the striking notes in her staccato passages to the fortississimo sections loud as a rock concert to soft pianissimo sections where the sounds coming from the instrument are barely audible, Victoria used the keys to transfer emotions. Playing for her was a lived experience. Anyone listening felt the sounds down to their soul. She felt emotionally spent when finished, but she loved it that way. Her hands glided effortlessly across the keys as she played her favorite piece, *Moonlight Sonata.* The keys of her ten-foot Fazioli concert grand responded with precision to her every touch.

Victoria had a special connection to this instrument. When she was eleven, her father took her to Italy to pick out a piano and help design some custom features on it. Together they selected a traditional high polish ebony finish with an inlaid mother-of-pearl *VH.* When the handmade piano was finished, they made the return trip to approve it before shipping it to the U.S. They each affixed their signature with a date to the soundboard as a way to capture the special moment in time. Victoria remembered fondly playing it in the factory while all the craftsmen looked on.

Her father told her how proud he was. Now, this is one of the few things she had left in the house that she treasured. Her mother had, over the years since his death, unceremoniously stripped the compound of anything precious to her father. Any remembrances had been discarded like Tuesday's trash. She hated her mother for that and as the memories returned she lost track of her place in the music. In frustration, she slammed her fists onto the keys, making a terrible sound that resonated within the music room. She sat there for a minute, lost in thought until she heard a sound behind her.

"Victoria, dear. Why did you stop playing? It sounded so lovely."

The sound startled Victoria as she swiveled around on the bench to see her mother sitting on a chair behind her. "You should announce yourself, Mother. Slinking around like a cat in the night is unbecoming of you."

"I didn't want to disturb you. You know how much I enjoy hearing you play," Mrs. Van Hough said, and her voice sounded sincere to most. But Victoria heard the contempt. She hated this piano, and when Victoria played, it reminded her of her late husband. She would have gotten rid of it years ago, but she knew Victoria would never have forgiven her. So she tolerated it, rarely stepping foot into the music room. But she had made an obvious exception this morning, and Victoria was curious to find out why. She didn't ask, instead she chose to wait for her mother to reveal her intentions. The chess match was on. Again.

After a minute of awkward silence, Victoria tired of waiting. She knew she wasn't especially good at this game and didn't really care. "You haven't been in this room in at least six months. To what do I owe the pleasure of your company, Mother?"

"Hmm. Right to the point, I see. Just like your father," she said disapprovingly. Victoria knew that invoking her father's name was a sure way to push her buttons, but she tried to stay strong and not respond. She turned back to the piano to hide the anger in her face and began fiddling with the keys. "Ever since you returned from Peru, you have been a bit distant. Is everything okay?"

Victoria thought this comment was strange since it showed her cards so soon. Usually her mother liked to string her along more. She loved to keep her guessing until the last minute, then spring the trap on the unsuspecting person. "Everything is fine. Why do you ask?"

"Well, it's just that I've heard Dr. Morris's son has tried to contact you several times without success. Why aren't you returning his calls?"

"I'm sure I've made myself clear on this. I'm not interested."

"Oh, Victoria, dear, he's a wonderful young man. Harvard educated, you know," she said trying to sweeten the pot, but Victoria stayed quiet. Finally, she took out her dagger. "He's gone you know."

Victoria sat up straight and spun around to look at her mother. "What are you talking about?" She saw a smile cross her mother's face, knowing she had her attention now.

"Just as I thought. You really haven't spoken to him, have you?"

"Mother, I'm not up for your riddles today."

"I thought I would share the disappointing news with you that poor Mr. DeFranco is heading out of town today. In fact, he's probably already gone." Victoria could feel her heart breaking. But she knew her mother couldn't be trusted to tell the truth, especially if it was in her best interests.

"I'm guessing that if it's true, you had something to do with it."

"Oh, no dear. Certainly not. I believe he finally realized he's out of his league. Or more accurately, *you* are out of his league. He'll be much happier now, free to pursue someone in his social class. And, as luck would have it, so will you."

Victoria's mind was racing with questions. Was he really leaving? Why didn't he tell her? Was their relationship over? The more she ran these questions in her head, the more anxious she got. She fidgeted on the bench, refusing to look at her mother.

Her mother stood up and walked over to the piano, running her hands along the edge. She wanted to see Victoria's face when she began the last act of her play. "By the way, I decided to make a donation to his foundation after all. Quite a generous one, if I do say so. He was pleased."

Like the first domino in a string that started the others falling in succession, so, too, did this comment begin the act of understanding for Victoria. She was connecting the dots. Her mother could see it in her eyes and she was pleased. No, not pleased. Victoria thought she read excitement on her mother's face. Her anger rose.

"Really? I didn't think his work impressed you."

"Not at all, but I'm willing to give him a chance to prove me wrong."

"You would never have given anyone money unless you could see the look on their face in person. Where did you meet him?" The words weren't even out of her mouth when the next domino fell. "I was in Peru. That trip came up at the last minute. How convenient." Her feelings of betrayal were boiling over inside.

"Yes, convenient indeed. Who could have predicted that?" Her mother smiled a devious smile.

"You bought him off, didn't you?" Victoria said as her voice rose, and her face flushed. As she looked at her mother, she couldn't believe what she was seeing. Her mother looked like a small child on Christmas morning as she opened presents. With each revelation the paper was torn back and the present became more identifiable. "You paid him to not talk to me!" Another domino.

"Oh, Victoria, if it were only that easy. I merely made a generous donation. If he isn't talking to you, it's a choice he has made with no input from me. But I must admit, you are so much better off."

"I can't believe you paid him off, Mother. You are the

epitome of evil."

"No, darling. Love is not evil. What I'm demonstrating is love. You do whatever is necessary for the ones you love."

Then the last domino hit a table of Victoria's mind as the words came back to her. *He's probably already gone. You do whatever is necessary for the ones you love.* She would not let her win. She made a huge mistake by not going to see Marco, but she would correct that now.

"You won't win, Mother," she said with a calm confidence that surprised herself. She stood up and walked out of the room. Behind her, she heard her mother banging on the keys.

"Don't waste your time, Victoria! It's over!"

In Victoria's head she was telling herself it was definitely not over. She went from a fast walk to a run as she headed to the garage.

***

She yelled at the gate as it slowly opened. "Come on, come on!" She just cleared it by inches as she whipped the car around the corner and onto the road. The tires spun easily as she made the next turn, heading toward the interstate. It had been raining all day with temperatures near freezing. Water pooled all along the road, and her car slowed considerably when it hit each puddle, only to lurch ahead again on the other side. The deeper pools threw large amounts of water on her windshield, making it impossible to see for several seconds.

Even the doom and gloom of the day couldn't bring Victoria down. She was concerned about her mother's comments and her donation to Marco's foundation. And she wasn't sure if that had anything to do with why he hadn't responded to her calls or texts. What she knew was she thought she was in love with him. Over the previous week, she had lots of time to think about their future together. She had decided what course to take, and she was ready to tell

Marco.

As she merged onto the interstate, she pressed the accelerator. The engine of her Benz roared to life, quickly pushing the car to eighty. Weaving in and out of the cars, she knew she should slow down, but she couldn't. She had to get to him and tell him how she felt. She would never forgive her mother for interfering in her happiness. What did she know about love? Nothing. She was a bitter shrew who buried the best thing to ever happen to her. Then she danced on his grave. Victoria swore that she would never become her mother. Twenty-five minutes and she would be there. She hoped her mother was wrong about him being gone already, but deep down inside she knew the odds were not in her favor.

CHAPTER TWENTY-ONE
Marco

His back was killing him as he carried boxes through the house, out the front door and into the waiting Airstream sitting in the driveway. It had that new house smell and Marco stood in the doorway taking it all in. He never imagined how beautiful it could have been until he brought it home. It represented for him the start of his new life. He set the box down on the floor and took a seat on the sofa. He pulled out his wallet, opening it and pulling out a small photo. In it was a man and a young boy sitting on a bench together in a travel trailer. Their beaming smiles showed the excitement within them both. Marco stared at the photo and a tear escaped, running down his face.

"I did it, Dad. I just wish you were here to enjoy it with me. But I know you are here with me." He gave the photo a gentle kiss, pointed a finger to the sky, then replaced it in his wallet. No time for sentimentality. He still had work to do to get on the road today. He stood up and went back into his house to retrieve the last few boxes. Marco decided to wait to unpack his things until he got to his first destination. This represented a novel way of living for the ultra-organized person. Additionally, his itinerary was totally up in the air, which was new to him as well. Normally,

Marco wouldn't have considered leaving the driveway without the complete route having been mapped out, including fuel stops and bathroom breaks. He was trying to embrace his inner free spirit so all he knew was where he would stop the first night. After that, he was winging it. As he thought about it, and the lack of preparation, it caused him anxiety and a slight pain in his stomach, but he went with it anyway.

He placed the last two boxes on the floor of the Airstream. Slowly, he took one more walk around, making sure everything would travel safely; no boxes on the table or counters. It didn't take many bumps in the road before everything would have ended up scattered and broken on the floor. Satisfied that he wouldn't have any casualties, he moved to the door, stepped out, and closed it behind him. He fished the key out of his pocket and locked the door.

A noise from behind startled him. He was still gun-shy since his run-in with the thugs and found himself jumping at the slightest sound. He whirled around to see the source. Allison was walking down the driveway, and she had Harry, her boyfriend, in tow. Harry was a tall man with broad shoulders, a full beard, and long hair pulled into a ponytail. He was much older than Allison, but that didn't seem to matter to her, and Marco was glad that Allison had someone in her corner like him.

"All packed?" Allison asked as she got closer to Marco.

"Just locked her up. Let's do a final walk-through before I leave."

The three of them walked into the trailer and looked around. It was almost unrecognizable to Marco. The shelves were empty, as were the pantry cabinets and bathroom.

"I think that's everything," Marco said as he took one last look around. He took his key ring out and removed the house key. "This is for you, Allison." He handed the key over. "Thanks again for everything. Keep me updated with your life."

Allison held her arms out and got a hug from Marco

before he walked out and down the driveway to his truck. He unlocked the door and got in. The truck roared to life and Marco put it in reverse. When he arrived yesterday, he pulled in forward down the driveway. He didn't get any training regarding pulling a travel trailer safely. Now he had to back out. How hard could it be, he thought? He turned around to look out the back window but realized it was fruitless. All he saw out the rear window was a big chrome blob. Hmm. He faced forward and started backing up. Immediately, the trailer lurched left, so he turned the wheel to correct it. "Damn, wrong way," he said as the trailer headed off at an awkward angle made worse by Marco. He put the truck in drive and moved forward to straighten it out. "Try that again," he said. Back he went again. This time the trailer went right, and he overcorrected as the trailer appeared to snake down the driveway. Suddenly he heard a voice. "STOP!" and Marco slammed on the brakes. He put the truck in gear, went around behind the trailer to see Harry standing there.

"Dude, you almost clipped the house," he said, and pointed along the blind side of the trailer. Marco peeked around the corner and saw he was definitely right. He stopped just in time. He shook his head and returned to the truck, pulling forward to straighten things out.

This time, he was determined to take it much slower. The possibility of damaging his two-day-old trailer made him nervous, and much more cautious. He put the truck in reverse one more time and slowly backed up. With slight course corrections and the help of Harry's booming voice, Marco crept down the driveway. "Turn left. Now right. No! Your other right!" With only a one-bush casualty, Marco was finally in the street, ready to depart on his new adventure. He suddenly noticed the large pit in his stomach and knew, deep down, why it was there. Victoria. But he was doing what he needed to do to keep her safe and to keep himself from suffering the wrath of her mother.

He waved to Allison and Harry, put the truck in drive,

and headed out of the cul-de-sac. He turned right, but as the trailer followed around the corner, it ran up onto the curb. Marco swore under his breath, realizing it was going to take some time before he could safely navigate the streets with his new home. He cautiously headed down the street and turned left on his way to the interstate and a southbound start to a new life.

CHAPTER TWENTY-TWO
Victoria

Victoria slowed her car to an almost-safe speed as she headed down the off-ramp before stopping at the first traffic light. She had to be careful since the snow was sticking, making travel much more dangerous. The light turned green, and she sped away through the intersection, never seeing the brand-new truck and chrome travel trailer that waited in the turning lane to merge onto the interstate heading south.

She was nearly there and prayed feverishly that Marco was still home. One more right turn, then down the cul-de-sac to the end, but her heart dropped when she saw the driveway was empty. She stopped and looked around to see if she missed something in her haste. Nothing. Certainly nothing like that chrome beast she saw in his calendar. She eased off the brake and headed down the driveway next to what was now Marco's former home.

Snow was falling faster now, and it was sticking to everything. Victoria got out of her car and dashed to the door. Maybe he hadn't picked it up yet, right? If he was gone, she couldn't imagine a worse ending to her day. Then she heard the door open and saw Allison standing there.

"Oh crap," both women said in unison, then laughed

uncomfortably.

"Hi, Allison, right?" Victoria started as Allison nodded her head. Victoria had never met Allison and was glad to finally see the woman who Marco had relied on so much. But she wished the meeting was taking place under better circumstances. Victoria was on a mission now and didn't want to waste a minute on small talk. "Is Marco here?"

"I'm sorry, Victoria, he's not. He left just before you got here."

"Damn! Do you know where he's going?" Victoria asked with panic creeping up in her voice.

"He was headed south on the interstate. Down there." She pointed in the direction where Victoria just came. "You'll have to hurry if you want a chance to catch him." Allison's words echoed in her head. *HURRY!* She spun around, moving swiftly to the driver's side of her car. As she opened the door, Allison called out to her.

"I don't know if this makes a difference or not. I think you should know that Marco's in love with you."

"Thank you. That means a lot to me," she responded, feeling dread at the thought that she may not be able to reach him. Across the snowy divide, in a statement of great irony, the first person whom Victoria openly professed her love for Marco was Allison. "I love him, too."

She ducked down into the car, closed the door, and started the engine. Without taking time to brush off the accumulating snow from her windows, she backed out of the driveway and sped down the slushy snow-covered streets headed to the interstate. She had no idea how far ahead he was or if she could catch him. But she had to try. How exactly she would get him to stop hadn't even crossed her mind yet.

The light turned green, and she sped up the entry ramp and into southbound traffic. Her car fishtailed as she changed lanes, dodging vehicles as she went. Her wipers cleared away large flakes of snow, but she still couldn't see more than a few cars ahead of her. As the miles and minutes ticked by, she wondered if she would ever find him. She reached up to her face and wiped away a tear. But Victoria was a fighter, and she refused to give in to those feelings. She pressed the accelerator farther, speeding off in search of her destiny.

CHAPTER TWENTY-THREE
Marco

Under normal circumstances, this would have been a beautiful day. It was a crisp early winter day. The trees were covered in fresh, white snow and being pushed back and forth by a stiff wind. But Marco wasn't able to appreciate any of this. He had his hands full trying to keep his new truck and 4,000-pound chrome bullet on the road. He had zero experience towing a trailer, and he wondered if he was in over his head. *How can they just hand you the keys and send you on your way with no training?* he said to himself. When he picked out his dream Airstream, it seemed logical to him. Not anymore. And the snow wasn't helping, either. With every gust of wind, the Airstream trailer swayed back and forth in an almost uncontrollable motion, creating a serpent trail along the snow-covered interstate. They advised Marco to stay in the right lane, and he considered that an excellent suggestion. As the large trucks passed on his left, they sucked him into their wake and he fought to keep from hitting them. He wasn't sure what he would have done if they were on both sides. He wasn't making good time, but that didn't matter to him. Forward progress was all that mattered. Onward toward his new life and happiness. Frequently he questioned how happiness could be possible without Victoria, but he brushed those thoughts aside. He would deal with that later.

His first stop was in 210 miles, and he began doing the calculations in his head to determine the time of his arrival. There, he would stop for the night. The first night in his trailer. Hopefully by morning, this early winter snowstorm would be past and most of the snow would have melted off the streets.

His attention, which had been momentarily diverted from the roads, was quickly returned when a car went flying by him, throwing large chunks of dirty snow and slush onto his windshield, temporarily blinding him. Marco slowed the truck, and the wipers swept by, clearing his vision again. "Damn crazy drivers! They make this even more difficult than it has to be," he said as he brought the truck back up to speed. The car that caused the commotion sped past him, but Marco noticed the brake lights had come to life and the car was slowly coming back to him. Maybe they were going to apologize, Marco thought. He would rather have had them just continue on their way instead.

Marco gained on the car until it was even with his side window. He was annoyed now. Why didn't they just go? Suddenly, the driver of the car began honking the horn. What was going on? Snow had accumulated on part of his side window and the view was further obscured by fog. He wiped the fog away and tried to see who was honking. He didn't know why they were acting this way. He had done nothing wrong.

Honk! Honk! There was something frantic about the noise. Marco rolled down his window as the passenger-side window of the car rolled down, too. Because his truck sat so much higher than the car, he couldn't see who was driving. The honking continued and Marco wondered if something was wrong with his trailer. Maybe a door had opened or a window. It was possible that a tire could be going flat. Could this person be a Good Samaritan, warning him of a problem that needed immediate attention? Now

Marco was concerned. He began scouting for a spot where he could pull over to check. He slowed down and eased the truck and trailer off the interstate onto the wide, slush-covered shoulder. After putting the truck in park, Marco set the parking brake before putting his jacket on. Cars and trucks went flying by at highway speed, and Marco made a mental note to be extra careful when getting out. He checked the mirror but because of the snow and fog on the window, couldn't see anything. When it seemed safe, Marco opened the door, jumped to the ground, and ran right into Victoria, nearly knocking her into oncoming traffic.

"Oh my God! Victoria, I'm so sorry! Are you okay? How did you get here?" Marco was astonished to see her on the side of the highway and hadn't figured out how she got there. Victoria jumped into his arms, catching Marco totally by surprise, and held him tight. He had been missing this so much. Often, over the past few weeks, he had yearned to feel her in his arms and to hold her close. Now she was here. He wrapped his arms around her and held her in a warm embrace. But Marco was jolted back to the reality of their surroundings when a car sped by, splashing slush and ice onto them, up to their waists. Victoria looked down at her high heels, now full of water, and they both let out a laugh. Snow continued falling and had already left a dusting of large flakes on them both.

"Victoria, why are you here?" Marco asked, having to raise his voice to be heard over the traffic whizzing by.

"At first, I couldn't understand why you weren't calling me back, but now I know. My mom can be extraordinarily evil. I know she paid you to stay away from me."

"She did more than that. She threatened me. I felt like my safety was at risk. I'm sorry, Victoria, but I didn't want you to be put at risk, too. As irrational as she was, I was worried that you would be in danger, too. I wasn't willing to take that chance." Her hands were still holding onto Marco's as they talked in this most inhospitable environment. Most drivers saw their vehicles stopped on the side and give them plenty of room. Not all. Several cars continued throwing dark, dirty slush onto them and by this time, their lower halves were soaked. But it seemed, from Marco's perspective, not even this could dampen Victoria's enthusiasm.

"I know how my mother is. We can't let that affect us. We have to live our lives and Marco, I want that to include a life with you."

"What about the money?" Marco asked, thinking back to the night of the fundraiser. He took the money, knowing Victoria would never forgive him. How could she? And he knew Mrs. Van Hough would tell her. It was her trump card. Paid in full, providing another wedge between them. Marco rationalized that he didn't think he had a choice. Regardless, he still took it.

"I'm so sorry, Marco! I can't even imagine what she did and said to you that night. I'm sure she made it as intimidating as possible, and I'm sure you felt like you had no choice. But the money helped you buy your dream and start a new life, and I want to be a part of that!"

"You think I actually used that money? You think I spent your mother's hush money to buy my dream?" Marco asked with disbelief. "How could I? By taking that money, I was agreeing to never talk to you again. I was heartbroken. But what choice did I have?"

"I don't understand. What did you do with the money, then?"

This was a subject he never thought he would discuss with her, but now, on the side of the interstate, on a snowy winter day, he disclosed some important information.

"I gave it away."

"Wait, you did what?"

"I donated it to the homeless shelter. We used it to create an endowment for that and two other shelters in the area. They will have enough money to pay their expenses for years to come." Marco waited for the words to land on Victoria and her to react to them. "And we called it the Alice

Van Hough endowment fund," he finished with a smile.

While still holding his hands, she began to jump up and down, slush splashing everywhere. The sight made Marco laugh. "That's brilliant, Marco!" she shouted. "You made something good come out of this. That's why I..." She stopped talking and bouncing and eased into his arms again, her mouth by his ear. "That's one of the many reasons why I have fallen in love with you, Marco DeFranco." She pulled her face away from his and looked him in the eyes. "I know it's crazy. Sometimes it seems like the entire world is against us. It seems reckless to do this, but I believe we should love each other recklessly. Without abandon. Without regard for anything else around us or anyone else. I don't know what will happen in the future. My mother is capable of wicked things. But I don't care. I'm hopelessly in love with you."

Marco stared into her eyes the way he did when they first met in the coffee shop. It seemed like it was so long ago. Then, like now, he was lost in them. So beautiful. Marco saw how beautiful she was, both inside and out. Everything around them just melted away as he enjoyed this moment with her.

The sound of an air horn filled the air as a tractor trailer approached. Instinctively, Marco grabbed Victoria, spun her around, and shielded her against his truck. As the tractor trailer passed, its horn sounded again and slush sprayed up over the top, completely coating Marco. He held her tight. This was exactly where he wanted to be. He wanted to protect her, be with her, and love her. Marco released his grip on her and looked once again into her eyes and told her, "I want to spend my days protecting you and keeping you safe. I want to be the partner you are searching for." And for the first time in his adult life, he told a woman, "Victoria... I love you." She melted into his arms, and he knew they were both filled with excitement and hope. They both believed that whatever happened, they would overcome it. They kissed one last time, a sweet kiss between two people who had finally found love. Afterward, Marco led her safely back to her car before taking his place behind the wheel in his truck. He let out a sigh. Not a sigh of frustration, but one of new love. He was hooked, and there was no turning back now. He looked at the passenger seat and imagined Victoria sitting there with her beautiful smile beaming back at him, and he couldn't wait.

Marco put the truck in drive and led them back onto the snowy road. Planning for their future was an activity best done in a safer environment, and he couldn't wait to get started. For the first time, he was going to be taking someone else's needs and wants into consideration, and that thought excited him. They would work as a team and make a new life together in California. But Marco knew that in order for them to have any chance of succeeding, there was some unfinished business that needed to be resolved. Instead of exiting onto the interstate heading west, he took the route that led them back toward town.

The End

For now…

AFTERWORD

Thank you so much for reading my book! I hope you enjoyed it. If so, maybe you would consider doing me a favor. Reviews matter to authors like me. Please leave a review for me.

If you are interested in getting information about upcoming release dates for future books in this series or others, or if you would like to learn more about me or subscribe to my newsletter, visit my website at:

http://www.raemerson.com

You can connect with me by sending an email here:

info@raemerson.com

Thank you again!!

ABOUT THE AUTHOR

Hi! My name is Robert Emerson, and I love writing Contemporary Romance novels. But it wasn't always about writing. In fact, being an author is one of many careers I've enjoyed during my working life. Over that time, I've worked as a cook, a printer, an Operations Manager and a Registered Nurse to name just a few. Each job has helped me create a rich pool of experiences that I can draw from to write deep and engaging characters. I'm a romantic at heart and enjoy writing stories of love, trial, betrayal and redemption.

For the last few years, I have lived with my wife, in a 320 square foot tiny house on wheels. We travel the country, seeing beauty around us, and of course, I use these experiences to enhance my novels. We have five children between us who are all grown adults. Instead of pets, we have a cactus.

I love hearing from my readers so feel free to drop me an email, sign up for my newsletter or follow me on social media. Thank you all!

www.ingramcontent.com/pod-product-compliance
Lightning Source LLC
Chambersburg PA
CBHW070650100726
47907CB00007B/2157